IT'S EASY TO FALL ON THE ICE

Ten Stories by

ELIZABETH BREWSTER

IT'S EASY TO FALL ON THE ICE

Some of these stories have already appeared in *Canadian Forum*, *Dalhousie Review*, *Fiddlehead*, *Journal of Canadian Fiction* and *Quarry*. "It's Easy to Fall on the Ice" was published in *Stories from Atlantic Canada*, edited by Kent Thompson. The author is grateful to the Canada Council for a Senior Arts Award, which enabled her to complete work on this collection.

ISBN 0 88750 247 4 (hardcover)
ISBN 0 88750 248 2 (softcover)

Design: Michael Macklem

Printed in Canada

PUBLISHED IN CANADA BY OBERON PRESS

For Don and Frances and Phyllis and Reg

VISITING HOURS

It did not seem at all strange to visit Luke in the hospital; quite usual, in fact, though she had never been there before. She stopped at the reception desk and asked if she could see Luke Henderson, and the girl handed her a card with his name on it and the number of his room in the medical ward. She walked down the antiseptic-smelling corridor, took the wrong turning at some point (but she would have done that even if she had visited it before: she was always taking wrong turnings), was directed down another corridor, and finally found the room. The door was open, and she walked in. Luke was sitting propped up in bed, looking a little pale but otherwise quite normal, considering that he had nearly died since the last time she had seen him. It was already several weeks since his heart attack. He said, "Hi, Alice" to her rather flatly. The carnations she had ordered from the florist were on his bedside table. They caught her eye, and she thought them a little too ornate. She tiptoed into the room, feeling as though she must not get too close to someone who had been in danger and might be again. She sat down, half gingerly, on the chair beside his bed.

Has she come back to take me over? he thought. Because if she's come back to take me over she certainly isn't going to. And yet in a way he was glad to see her. He had only been in Charlestown for a year. He had no relatives here and few friends. Possibly she was not a friend. Possibly she wanted to be a relative, and her wanting to be a relative was a threat to him. But, after the visits of people who called on him as a duty, there was something faintly comforting in the visit of someone who really wanted to see him.

"Why don't you sit on the bed?" he asked. "Don't you want to be near me?"

"I thought it was against hospital rules," she said, getting up from the chair and perching on the foot of the bed. The bed was high and she was too short to sit on it easily. What she meant was that she was afraid he didn't want her there. After all, the last time she had been in Charlestown, in May, they had not got on very well. She had, she supposed, thrown herself at him and he had rebuffed her, and she had wept copiously and told him that it didn't matter, she didn't love him anyway. But then, after that, he had said how lonely he was and they had agreed to go out together after she had come back. She had gone down to the States to finish her degree at summer school; and then while she was away she had a letter from his landlady saying that he had

had the heart attack and asking her to write to him although he couldn't write to her yet. And finally he had written to her, and she began to feel that perhaps he had not meant to rebuff her before. Because after all he was the one who had suggested—hadn't he?—that she might come back to Charlestown to work.

They had got to know each other the year before, when she had been in Charlestown for the summer and he had just come there. They had eaten their lunches together at the Campus Hut, sitting in one of the dingy booths and hearing the juke-box blare in the background while they exchanged the stories of their lives. They had strolled about the campus or sat reading poetry together in the park by the fountain. They had gone to the little movie house together and watched the Wild West banging across the screen in the almost deserted house. They had gone for long walks together on dusty country roads or along the railway track. She had given him tea and cookies in her landlady's kitchen, enjoying the domesticity of washing up together afterward. She had liked him because he seemed relaxed and easy, not particularly ambitious, not particularly emotional. She had liked him also because he had asked her many questions about herself, and she was not used to people being interested in her. She had always considered herself, apologetically, as being rather mousy. Objectively, she knew this was not true. She created a kind of mousiness almost by design, so that people would not observe her; but the habit of fading into the background was so well established for her that she could not bring herself out of the background when she wanted to be noticed. But Luke did not think she was mousy, though he observed her habit of fading. Her eyes were too large, dark, and intelligent for that. Her tongue, also, was too sharp. He wasn't sure, as a matter of fact, that she wasn't a little bit dangerous. If she really wanted to take him over there might be a hard struggle.

"You don't seem at all surprised that I'm here," she said.

"I'm not. I expected you to come. I've been expecting you. I liked your cards."

She had sent him several sick cards—sick sick cards—and they were carefully propped up beside the flowers and the glass of fruit juice on the table. Also, a book she had sent him lay open on the bed.

She searched around in her mind for something to say. He had always been easy to talk to, but now she was not sure. One must not disturb someone who has just had a heart attack, or argue with him, or worry him. She did not think she could ever be comfortable with him again until she had talked to him about the trouble on the last visit. But she could not see how that could be mentioned until he was well, and that might be months away. She felt almost angry with him for being ill. She had always disliked people who had to be handled with kid gloves, knowing that her own gloves were not too smooth. She had liked him because he seemed in vigorous physical and emotional health and did not need to be treated with any false tenderness. And now he had proved her wrong by having this silly heart attack.

He wondered what she was thinking. He had thought to begin with that she was quite honest, once one had passed her first stiff little defenses. She seemed rather eager to say what was on her mind. He had really liked her that first summer, had found her almost lovable. There was a pleasure in drawing her out, in being drawn to a certain extent in return. But she was not a letter writer. The letters he had received from her the year she was away were not particularly revealing, were hardly more than polite. And people change in a year. He had changed, and he felt she didn't like the change. She had changed, and would probably not admit that she had changed. Then there was the business of coming back to Charlestown to work. She had written that she did not particularly like her job in Illinois. He had written back that there was a vacancy here, and first thing he knew it was settled that she was coming back, and everyone—some people, anyway—seemed to think it was on his account. Was it on his account? Because if it was, he would not have it. The vacancy had been there, and he had suggested it, but he had not seriously thought she would come back. She didn't particularly like the Maritimes, although she was a Maritimer. But that made it all the more likely that she had come back on his account. And he simply would not have it.

They sat in the hospital room talking about the view of the tide from his window, about his landlady's romance with the French professor, about the new grocery store opposite the post office, about her thesis, which she had not quite finished. In the midst of a silence, because she had nothing else to say, she took a poem out of her purse and handed it to him. This was in order. This was a relief. "I like it," he said, when he had read it through twice, "but I wish you weren't so concerned about technique. You're always fussing about technique."

"Am I?" she asked. She was pleased to be told that she was too concerned about technique, because she really thought she didn't take enough care with it.

There were footsteps outside the door, a man's footsteps and the high-heeled click of a woman's pumps. It was the head of the English Department and his wife, George and Andrea. Alice caught up the poem and put it away in her purse. Luke observed her with annoyance. As though the poem were a bloody love letter, he thought, which it wasn't.

Andrea could never be accused of mousiness. She was large and overwhelming in a rather stylish way. "Except for the wolf bit, she's rather like the Assyrian swooping," Alice thought. She even had on a glittering dress.

Still, they talked rather pleasantly, except that Andrea was heavy-handed in hinting—no, not hinting, positively saying—that Alice's presence was all that was needed for Luke's recovery. "Now that you're back he won't have anything to fret about," she said. Alice felt as though she were being ordered to marry Luke immediately to cook him hot nourishing meals and see that he looked after himself. Not that she would mind, really, but what did Luke think of all this?

This suits her, Luke thought. This suits her line. She can marry me to look after me. She can flatter herself that I need her. And the neighbours will say what a good thing it is for both of us, how lucky I am to get a good woman who will look after me and how lucky a mousy little girl is to get a man at all. I don't need anyone to look after me, and she isn't a mouse.

He tried to remember exactly what had happened, what had been said, on her visit in May. The trouble was that the heart attack had been almost like a mental breakdown. He could only remember foggily what had happened in the few months preceding it. He had met her bus, he remembered. She had seemed in quite high spirits, really gayer than he remembered her, though even so perhaps a little checked because he was not as gay as she remembered him. He had taken her out to dinner, to a motel a little outside the town. She had looked out the window at the fields and pastures, just beginning to be green with spring, and had half sighed with happiness, as though she were coming home. And to him, too. She thinks everything is going to be just the same, he had thought. But it couldn't be. "I'm just taking you out as a representative of the College," he had said with a smile. "You can take me seriously the next time I ask you out."

"Oh, yes, the next time," she had said, apparently unaware that he was not joking. "Anyhow, you've already taken me out lots of times. I suppose those times were terribly serious."

He felt tangled in what she had said, as though she had won a move in a game. Perhaps she had. But she had not won him. Nor had she won him now, visiting him in hospital with her apparent—or possibly real—solicitude.

Of course he had taken her out the next day. It was Sunday—a dark, cold spring Sunday—and they had driven around the back country roads. She had a taste for landscape. There was something of the nineteenth-century romantic about her. She liked these bleak marshes, the contrasting lines of woods, the ramshackle farm houses, the ruined graveyard where they got out and took snapshots of each other among the tombstones. He did not really like these places. He would rather have been somewhere more gentle and civilized, and he felt out of sympathy with her air of delighted homecoming.

George was wandering on now about some new novel he had been reading, and Alice was listening to him, looking bored. Alice could never manage to look interested when she wasn't. There was nothing of the actress about her. Or was there?

Alice remembered a line she had written once in a poem she had never finished.

Words are only
Pick-axes chipping at the block of silence.

Here we are, she thought, talking and talking and not saying anything. Silence is all around like a big block of ice, even if it is August. And it had been a bigger, icier block that time in May. She had so looked forward to seeing Luke again. She had hoped it would be possible to go on as if she had never been away. But she had felt strain and strangeness coming over her, a lack of warmth in the welcome. What's wrong? she had kept wanting to cry out. What's wrong? Why aren't things like they used to be?

But she hadn't cried out, anyhow not in words. She had rather enjoyed that day wandering around graveyards and looking at the Strait. She had a room with his landlady, who had been her landlady, and came downstairs and ate supper in his little kitchen with his landlady's cat purring at her feet. It cleared off in the evening and they drove out to a lake outside the town and sat and talked in the car.

That was when she had thought of words and pick-axes, because there was no sense of intimacy in spite of the appearance. Luke was talking about existentialism, about history, and she was not listening to him. She felt a giddiness in her head, as though the top would come off. "I'm trying to give you a little of my own philosophy, my own thought, and you aren't paying any attention to me," Luke said angrily.

"I'm not?" she said. "I'm not?"

She made a tremendous, an overwhelming effort, not moved by desire (because she was too dismayed by what she was doing to feel desire) but by the painful necessity of communicating in some other way than by words, and dropped—no, pushed—her head onto his shoulder and put her hand up to stroke his cheek. She felt that he was surprised, and at the same time she was surprised that he was surprised.

It was painful enough to have made that advance even if it had been accepted (because after all surely he should have made it first? Surely he was not really surprised?) but to have made the advance and had it rejected—that was what was really painful, what had made her burst into tears afterward and cry on his shoulder while she told him that she didn't really love him. She had made a great resolve that night not to be hurt, not to be angry, not to think it was of any consequence and not to speak of it to him again. And now she wished she had spoken of it to him again, because she wondered what picture of her was in his mind, and she could not speak of it to him now until he was well again, if she ever could at all.

Now Andrea was talking about her children. She was very fond of her children, and sorry for people who did not have any. "Do your brothers have children, Luke?" she asked.

"No, Andrea," he said, smiling. "I have no brothers. As the novels would say, I am the last of my name."

"Oh, well, Luke, you should do something about that."

"So I should, Andrea. What about that, Alice? Are you listening, Alice?"

She smiled at him, thinking that if he was fond of her it was a pleasant enough joke but if he wasn't it was not very kind.

She closed her eyes and wondered if she could communicate without saying anything out loud. "Dear Luke," she thought, forming the words clearly in her mind. "Are you really all that mad at me because I was lonely?"

THE CONVERSION

The year was 1953, the date a few days before Christmas. It was also a few days before Holly Dewar's twenty-fourth birthday; and, as she had been working in Ottawa for nearly a year without a visit home, she was looking forward to meeting her family on their farm near Fredericton.

Ottawa had not been as exciting as she had somehow expected it to be. She worked as a typist in a government office, surrounded by other similar girls. Her salary was not large, and in order to manage on it at all she had to keep constant track of expenses, adding them up in a little black notebook which she carried in her purse. She had a clean but claustrophobic room in the house of the genteel widow of a civil servant, Mrs. Murdoch. There was one other roomer, a kindergarten teacher in her early thirties. Holly prepared her own breakfast in Mrs. Murdoch's kitchen, and normally shared a dinner with Mrs. Murdoch and Lydia Duncan, the kindergarten teacher. She had lunch in the staff cafeteria with two or three of the other girls. She had met almost no men and had had only one date since coming to Ottawa, a depressing date with a creep named Al who kept telling her how many other girls wanted to go out with him.

It was good, then, after a dull year in Ottawa, to be lining up in Union Station for her seat on the train, carrying a fat suitcase with her clothes and presents and a handbag with a few books to read overnight. She was going coach class, as she could not afford a berth. She did not especially look forward to the trip, partly because she tended to get sick on trains, but it would be worth the discomfort to be home again.

The first part of the trip, as far as Montreal, was pleasant enough. She sat next to a middle-aged woman going to visit her married daughter for Christmas, and chatted with her now and then. When the woman was drowsing, Holly read a Graham Greene novel. She felt, in a way, like a character from a Graham Greene novel because she herself was in process of being converted—the only excitement of her year in Ottawa. In her bag were several more soberly Catholic books than the Greene novel, including a little catechism for inquirers; but she felt self-conscious about bringing them out when she was sharing a seat with another passenger.

Closing her eyes, she could see Father Cameron's office in the rectory, which she had been visiting once a week to take instruction. It seemed a foreign world, with its crucifix, carved figure of the Blessed Virgin, and portraits of Pope

Pius and lesser clergy. Her father, an old-fashioned New Brunswick Orangeman, would never, she feared, approve of those paraphernalia of an exotic faith. She herself was half repelled by them—they contrasted so much with the bare walls and plain doctrines of the Baptist Church that her parents attended—but she was also attracted. Rosaries and incense. The chanting of the Latin mass. The elaborate genuflections.

It wasn't just that, though—the strangeness, the tourist attraction. It was something more; and, now that she was on the train and had the whole night to think about it, she must decide what it was and whether she truly believed.

A going back to childhood belief, was it? Something miraculous, almost magical? Immortality absolutely true, a tangible fact? Sin and forgiveness, the sacraments. Eating salvation. Confession and absolution. Not that she had much to confess. Embarrassingly little, in a way. She wasn't a Great Sinner in the Graham Greene manner. Sex, she somehow gathered, was the chief possible sin, aside from eating meat on Friday. After all, she was not likely to murder anyone or forge a cheque, or even (since her mother had brought her up very strictly) speak a blasphemous word or two. But, as far as sex was concerned, men had never pursued her in any very whole-hearted way. Of course, as the catechism explained, you could sin by giving in to Impure Thoughts, and Thoughts were as real as Deeds. But less satisfying, somehow, even to confess.

Still, the great thing was not confession any more than it was incense or the rosary. Incarnation. That was it. The word become flesh. Spirit coming into the world, so that all those dead material things—houses, statues, government offices even—were transfused with spirit.

She had to change trains at West Montreal, and paced up

and down the platform in front of the small station waiting for her train to be called. It was a brisk, sparkling December evening, just pleasantly cold. The stars, high and yet somehow tender, lit up the dusting of snow on the ground and on the station roof. The people waiting for the train seemed to have a kind of Christmas sparkle about them as well. One nun in a black habit with a white pleated frill about her face seemed to Holly exceptionally beautiful and serene; but there seemed also to be a kind of serenity, a magic about the whole scene and all the people there.

Incarnation, she thought. The light shining in darkness. That's it. The whole world—the universe—all those stars out there—the nun's face—everything was the incarnation of the spirit. She wanted to cry with a sort of ecstasy of illumination.

She got on the train slowly, in something of a daze, lugging the suitcase. This train was more crowded than the other. She had to walk through several coaches before she came to one that had room, and it was a rickety old car, obviously brought out from retirement for the Christmas rush.

Just after she had settled down, a whole crowd of soldiers burst into the carriage. Back from Korea, they must be. The Korean war had ended in the summer, but soldiers were still arriving back. They were joyous, high-spirited, full of youth and animal vigour, some of them also full of more buyable stimulants. They took over most of the carriage, calling out to each other as they settled into their places and put up their rucksacks. Some of them looked in Holly's direction, but she put one of her books in front of her face in nervous self-protection, and they turned away from her, so that she kept her seat, and the seat directly opposite her, to herself.

Once they were settled down in their places, however,

she felt it was safe enough to observe them covertly. They too, like the Catholic Church, had the glamour of the unknown; you could even say that they were a sort of Order, a Secret Society, with a prescribed habit and a Communion of their own. Pretending to read, she listened with curiosity to their scraps of conversation, reminiscences of Korea, the strange country, fighting, girls they had known.

She turned again to her book. This one was an anthology of early Christian writers which she had bought in the Catholic bookstore downtown only last week. Before she had left Ottawa, when she was looking into it, it had seemed rather difficult and remote; but now, in the light of her recent illumination, everything seemed easy. Of course she believed. God, man, salvation, life, death, the universe, suffering—it all made sense. Any book she had picked up, even if it had been the Almanac, would have spoken to her in the same way. Like St. Augustine when he heard the children chanting, "Take, read," and picked up the scriptures, and there was the word, the very word, that he needed.

She was reading from Dionysius *On the Divine Names*: "Let us then press on in prayer, looking upward to the Divine benignant rays, even as if a resplendent cord were hanging from the height of heaven unto this world below, and we, by seizing it with alternate hands in one advance, appeared to pull it down. . ."

In her mind, just as it had on the station platform earlier, the light of the divine Rays illuminated everything, the railway car and the soldiers lolling in little groups. They too were clothed in Divinity, sacred, part of the Incarnation.

Four of them not quite directly across the aisle from Holly had been playing a card game, but had come to the end of a game and were bored. One of them, the good-looking tall boy who looked a little like Holly's cousin Matthew, leaned back and began to sing, and the others joined in. Army songs, drinking songs, sentimental love songs, some in foreign languages that Holly did not know. The tall boy was much the best singer of the group; he was also the one who had been drinking least. He sang joyously, in a warm tenor, with a sort of operatic fervour. Holly could not help turning her eyes toward him in half-acknowledged admiration.

As if he realized he was leading a performance for the benefit of a civilian audience, he turned to Christmas carols. Here he was sometimes the only one who knew all the words.

"You're showing off, Chris," one of his friends told him good-humouredly; yet they continued to join in the chorus as he led them through the "Twelve Days of Christmas."

Gradually the men became tired, stopped singing, drifted off to sleep. Young Chris continued to sing for a while by himself, finally concluding the little concert with "Adeste Fideles." Holly was surprised by the Latin words and surprised by the feeling, the hushed tenderness, with which he sang the hymn. He was looking in her direction when he finished, and she could not resist a slight, shy inclination of her head in acknowledgment of the pleasure she had felt.

With the singing over, and people settling down for the night, Holly's spirit of exaltation began to evaporate. The lights had been dimmed and she found it difficult to read. Also, the swaying of the train was finally beginning to make her feel sickish. She curled up on the seat and tried to sleep, but couldn't manage to. Restlessly, she shifted her position.

The conductor came by as she sat up.

"I think there's a seat vacant now a few cars up, Miss, if you find the boys too rambunctious," he said to Holly. "I could carry your bag."

Holly hesitated. The other car would probably be more comfortable. But she was feeling too nauseated to move.

"I don't feel very well," she told the man finally. "I don't think I want to walk that distance. It's quiet now anyway."

The conductor shrugged. "Suit yourself, Miss. I just thought you might be more comfortable, that's all."

He moved off to the next car, and Holly lay back again.

She opened her eyes when the young soldier, Chris, came back from the washroom and stood beside her with a paper cup in his hands.

"I heard you say you were sick," he said. "Would you like a drink of water?"

She shook her head. "I don't want anything to drink."

"It's just water. You don't think I've spiked it or something? Go ahead. It'll make you feel better."

After all, it was silly of her to refuse. He was just a kid, probably younger than she was, and he looked like Matthew. What harm could he do her? Just a nice kid, meaning to be kind.

And she did feel better, just a little, when she had drunk the water.

"You're going home to New Brunswick too?" he asked.

"Yes. Fredericton Junction. Or near there."

"Yeah? I'm from Saint John myself, but I have relatives in Fredericton. Will I ever be glad to see my folks. I hope we didn't disturb you with our little singsong?"

"No, it was fine, just fine. I enjoyed it," she said.

"Too bad you're not feeling well. Look, I bet this window would open. It's a real old carriage, before air conditioning. Do you want me to try?"

He tugged away at the window, and suddenly it opened and a blast of fresh air blew in from outside. Holly gulped the delicious cold and immediately felt less nauseated. She sat up straight and shook her head, clearing out the cobwebs.

Chris beamed. "Feel better? I knew that would help you."

She thanked him and smiled.

He lingered near her chair and said, "Would you mind if I sat here for a while? The others are all snoring away there, and I can't get to sleep. It passes the time to talk."

She hesitated. She did not want to be picked up. But he seemed a nice boy, not at all fresh, and he had sung "Adeste Fideles" with such feeling. Probably he was a Catholic. She nodded, a bit dubiously, and he sat down.

He began to talk, about Saint John, about his mother, who was a widow, about his army experiences, about Korea and his homesickness, the fighting, the ricefields, the girls. "You wouldn't believe how lonely I got sometimes," he said. "The other guys went out with the Korean girls, but I wanted some nice girl from home. And you wouldn't believe how much a guy needs someone gentle after fighting."

Some unspoken horror in the boy's eyes stirred Holly's pity. He did not move physically in her direction, but the air around them seemed to unite them in sympathy.

He fell silent, and they sat for a while without talking. Without the distraction of conversation, Holly was once more overcome by a slight feeling of nausea. She closed her eyes.

"Are you cold in that draught?" the soldier asked her solicitously. "Would you like my overcoat?"

She did not answer but he leaped up and brought his khaki army overcoat, which he wrapped gently around her, his hands touching her shoulders.

Again they lapsed into silence, but now Holly was conscious of his physical presence enveloping her, and her nausea departed. It was not a surprise when he reached out his hand, almost timidly, it seemed, and touched her hand. But surely there was nothing wrong in just holding hands for a while. It passed the time.

Eventually he shivered. "Do you mind if I share the overcoat?' he asked. "That's really a cold wind."

She did not answer, but she found him sitting close to her, with the coat nestling snugly around both of them. She ought not to have allowed this, she thought, but it seemed so peaceful. And she remembered at home on a sleigh ride, sitting close under a blanket with a boy, but that was all that happened.

His arm was around her now, and his fingers gently circled her breasts. The pressure was so light, it was as though butterflies were brushing her nipples. Nobody had ever done anything more than kiss her before, and that very clumsily. Sometimes she thought she would be an old maid and never be alive at all. A virgin over ninety years old, like that song one of her uncles sang. Her twenty-fourth birthday was so near. This butterfly pressure was reassuring. The hands were under her blouse, unfastening her bra, sweeping soothingly over her belly.

"I don't know your name," he whispered. "What's your name?"

"Holly. Holly Dewar."

"Chris and Holly. Both Christmas names. Kiss me, Holly."

She felt his tongue in her open mouth, and a flood of warmth went through her.

Feeling the searching hands stroking her thighs, she knew she should pull away now if she was going to, and she nearly did. But then a curiosity that seemed almost chilly overcame her. She wanted to know what the next move would feel like. Her mind, she thought, was calm and reasonable and in control. She would wait until the last possible moment and then she would pull away. But she ought not to wait. After all, she was in the midst of being converted. In her mind she began to repeat the Hail Mary, her attention only partly concentrated on the feel of the hands on her flesh.

It was at the point when he took her hand and guided it toward his open fly that she realized her control was not as perfect as she had thought. She gasped at the feel of the solid flesh, and pulled her hand away hastily. But not herself. She felt as though she were in a current being carried away from shore, and nothing could prevent her drift out into deep water.

Or so she thought. What prevented her continuing drift was that he moved too suddenly. She found herself all at once spun round, placed on her back with her legs jerked wide apart. She was startled back to herself, wrenched herself up and away. He let her go, gulped "Sorry," and turned to one side. She watched his solitary overwhelming convulsion with a mixture of feelings. She had never seen an orgasm before, and was terrified at the same time that she felt a kind of pride. Was it really herself, Holly Dewar, who had caused that turmoil? She could not be as sexless as she had feared.

There was no need now of moving. She knew instinctively that he would not touch her again. Soon he was asleep, his head fallen away from her, and she looked down curiously at his face. She was surprised that it was so remote and placid, almost as though carved out of marble, like the face of an archaic god. But she did not share his serenity. She must somehow calm herself, get rid of her panic trembling. She stared ahead of her, tidying her hair and trying to think of her conversion.

THE ESCAPE

For years, for almost all her life, Sophie Fanjoy had wanted to escape from the country. First—when she was Sophie Steeves—from her father's farm, the dilapidated old farmhouse, the smelly animals, all that dirt and deprivation she had grown up with. Then later from her husband's farm, cleaner and more prosperous, but narrow and claustrophobic, where she had felt dominated first by her husband's parents, then by his energetic elder sister, Addy, who had never married and had continued to live with them. Addy, who would be sure now to come to the hospital with Doug, their son Ronnie and his wife Linda. Not that Sophie minded now not having the chance to be alone with Doug. By this time he also seemed a part of the country that she wanted to escape from, one of the jailers who had used the word "love" to imprison her.

Well, now she had finally escaped from the farm. She was in town—not a large town, but town anyway. But she had come here to go to hospital. To die, as it turned out. At least she hadn't been fooled, as so many people were, about her chances for life. She liked to know facts, and Doug had not the self-control to keep them from her. He had, as she said to herself with mild disdain, carried on about it. Not that he was grieved for her, but for himself. "What will I ever do without you?" he kept saying. And he did not want her to be too heavily drugged when he visited because he wanted to be able to talk to her, to remind her again of how much he loved her, to ask her yet once more if she loved him too. Love. It was just that he was used to her, would find life uncomfortable without her. He didn't know the difference between love and need.

Lying in the hospital bed, she found it easy to let her mind drift back and back to her youth, to the time when she had really believed Doug loved her. Taken in by all those words. Taken in more by his good looks, his charm, the appeal of the healthy young animal in him. (Ronnie, her son, was like him. She felt sorry for Linda.) Thirty years ago, that was. Married before she was twenty. And now she was dying. Of cancer. Ugly word, which people didn't like to say. The growth is malignant, they said, instead.

She kept her eyes closed because if she opened them the old woman in the next bed would talk. A great chatterer, though deaf as a post. She wanted to tell Sophie about the visits of her children. Imaginary children. The poor woman had none of her own. Mrs. Harris, her name was, probably a sensible woman in her time, but between old age and the drugs she was taking she was suffering from softening of the brain.

The old woman looked a little like her own grandmother, who had kept house for her father after her mother had left. No wonder her mother had left him. A slouchy, unkempt, dirty man, always with a three-day bristle on his chin, smelling like his pigs. Doug wasn't like that, she had to give him credit. And a surly man, her father was. Not many words to spare, and half those were swear words. It was looking at her father, listening to her father, that had first made Sophie decide she must escape. And the ugliness of the farm, its discomfort. And the awful, ignorant neighbours. And the worst of it was that the neighbours were sorry for her. Poor, motherless Sophie Steeves, growing up with her no-good, grouchy father and her deaf old grandmother.

But Sophie would show the neighbours. Sophie would learn to sew and fix herself decent clothes. Sophie would memorize all her schoolbooks so that she could lead her classes. Somehow, Sophie would get away. First, to high school in the next small town, where she looked after the banker's children for her board.

Lucky that the War was on when she graduated from high school. Teachers were so scarce that she could teach for a year in a one-room school with a local licence. Then to Normal School in Fredericton. Her happiest year, or so she remembered it. Decorous tree-lined streets, sedate walks with her girlfriends on the Green, pretending to ignore the soldiers who tried to pick them up, window shopping in what seemed to her lavish shops.

The next year, the year the War was over, she came, aged nineteen, to take charge of the Hopedale School. She certainly had no intention of staying in Hopedale. She would save her money, go to summer school at university, get a degree, and teach high school in Fredericton or Moncton or Halifax. Maybe, finally, Toronto. But instead, because she boarded at the Fanjoys, she met Douglas Fanjoy, just back from the War. Happy-go-lucky, reckless, jovial (as he seemed then) Doug Fanjoy, who wasn't her type at all. But how she remembered that time. The feel of his hand on her bare arm the first time they danced together. Going skating with him, his arm around her waist.

Perhaps he wouldn't have noticed her if she hadn't been boarding in the same house. She wasn't his type either, she supposed. Too quiet a girl. But she had a cute figure. He would notice that. Maybe it was just that they saw each other every day. And, as for her, she hadn't been used to all that notice from a man. Men didn't usually pay her much attention. That was the only way she could excuse the fact that she had been so easy to get. Oh, and curiosity too. Her grandmother had told her so little about sex that she wanted to know what happened next. And nobody had told her it was so difficult, once you had got past a certain point, to say no. At least, to say no and mean it. And, once it happened, of course you thought it was love. If it wasn't love, how could you respect yourself?

Had it been the same for Ronnie's Linda? But Linda hadn't the same trouble growing up. Businessman's daughter from Toronto, sent to a Maritime university because that's where her mother had come from. Her parents hadn't forgiven her for taking up with Ronnie. Not good enough for them. A soft-handed girl then, though not now. Too clever and knowing; a bright, sharp little girl. (Then, not now.) But not so bright and sharp, at eighteen, that she hadn't got in the family way before she was married, the same as Sophie had. Ronnie just like his father. But maybe Linda had been clever. Maybe she had trapped him. Oh, that's what men always said. As though it wasn't just as much of a trap for a woman, more too. All those soppy diapers and curdled bibs and toilet training.

Trapped was how Sophie had felt, scared too, back when she had first realized Ronnie was on the way, when she missed her monthlies and was sick in the morning. The Fanjoys had thought she was lucky Doug had married her. Escape from one trap into another.

Involuntarily, she shifted in her bed now to drag herself out of the trap. When she opened her eyes Mrs. Harris was ready to pounce on her with questions. "Have you had a good nap, Mrs. Fanjoy? All ready for your family to visit? That good-looking husband of yours, such a fine man, and your son just like him."

Foolish to move, foolish to open her eyes, but after all she couldn't pretend forever to be asleep.

Tired. She would have been glad to hand her family over to Mrs. Harris when they came. Doug, large, bluff, red-faced, usually genial, now self-pitying. Addy, energetic and overpowering as always. Practical Addy, probably already calculating what the funeral would be like, how many relatives would come, what she would need to cook for supper after it was over. Ronnie, handsome as his father, but not so genial. A touch, just barely a touch, of surliness. Probably he felt trapped too, married young and working on the farm, when he had wanted to be an engineer. Linda, blonde and pale, shadows under her eyes, or was it just that make-up they wore now? Sophie eyed her figure carefully. Was she going to have another? But no—Linda would tell her right away, she wouldn't have to guess. "I'm pregnant, Mother Fanjoy," Linda would say, maybe in joy, maybe in despair, but she wouldn't keep it to herself, as Sophie would have done. Too plain-speaking, young people were now. Or were they? She wasn't sure. Really, she liked Linda, though she had to be critical of her.

Addy bustling, putting the flowers in fresh water, snipping their ends. Always wanting to be useful. "Keep still, Addy," Sophie wanted to say, but didn't. I never owned my own house, she thought. There was always Addy, after Doug's mother. Some people might have felt sorry for Addy, old maid sister in her brother's house, but they didn't know what Addy was like. Really the boss. Addy decided the colour of the kitchen wallpaper. Things like that.

Back in the early years of her marriage she had tried to persuade Doug to move away. Into town. Surely he could have got some other job than farming. Something in an office. But for all his bluffness and geniality, he didn't have the courage to face the town, lacked the training for it. Sometimes he would say, "Yes, later on. The old people need us now." But when the old people were gone, she and Doug had become the old people. She and Doug and Addy.

Once, early on, she had left for nearly a year. That was when Ronnie was three years old. Suddenly she felt she just couldn't stand it any longer, being looked down on by the old people and Addy and the neighbours, expected to feel grateful because Doug had married her. By then she realized that she and Doug shared nothing except the physical act of love, and even that seemed routine, perfunctory. She couldn't bear it when he got up after making love and lit his pipe. As if he needed that too. It was not that he didn't talk to her, but that what he said seemed (she had to admit) boring.

She went off and got a one-room school, taught for a year. But she had been worried about Ronnie, remembered what it was like to grow up without her mother. And Doug had come for her and talked her into going back. At least things were a little better after she came back. He didn't throw it up to her any longer that she had trapped him. No, now he needed her. And she didn't love him any longer. Not loving him made things easier, in a way. She could concentrate on Ronnie, and, later, on the little girl, Elsie.

But Elsie had died when she was five years old, of polio. She had no daughter. Maybe she could have talked to a daughter, as she couldn't to Doug or Addy or Ronnie. Or Linda. Linda now standing uncertainly by her bed, smiling at her questioningly. "Do you feel better today, Mother Fanjoy?" There was still something faintly childlike and wistful about Linda. Nervous in the presence of illness. She was sucking a thumb, biting a nail, without realizing what she was doing. Poor child. Not a child. She must be nearly thirty now. Why, Sophie thought, did I suppose once she was so much in control?

"As well as I'm likely to feel, Linda," she said. That probably sounded cold. Linda thought she was cold, she knew. But she wasn't. I'm not cold, Linda, she would have liked to say, but did not know how to say it.

The trouble was, she felt guilty toward Linda, because she thought Linda was living her own life over, and she didn't know how to save her from it. What could she do? The two men sitting there with their pale hair bleached by the sun, their startling blue eyes, their heavy masculinity. Ronnie sullen, Doug anxious.

"That's my girl," Doug said, patting her hand sentimentally. "Is there anything you'd like us to bring you?"

"No, nothing. Some grapes maybe."

If he could bring back her youth, the years between. Impossible. All those years she had nagged at him to get away; then the years when she thought, "Once Ronnie and Elsie are grown up, I'll leave." Then, "Once Ronnie is grown up." But by the time Ronnie had grown up she herself had lost her courage. She was an older woman without much training for a really good job, not in comparison with all those new bright young creatures like Linda or Linda's younger sister. Well, she had done her best. She had taught some years in the consolidated school in the next town, now that the old one-room schools had been closed. And she had saved a fair part of her salary from teaching. Why should she spend her money on the house? Addy's house, after all. Doug made enough from the farm. He wasn't a bad farmer, to be fair to him, though it was Addy's energy that carried him along.

So there was this money in the bank, which she had saved. For what? For a trip, maybe. A trip around the world. She had always wanted to see far places, Calcutta maybe, Rome or Athens, Jerusalem. Now she would never take the trip. And she must do something with the money.

"There is something," she said. "Could you send Charlie Groat in to see me, tomorrow if he could?"

So they would know she was making her will.

Unnecessary, Doug would think. Who could she leave the money to except Doug and Ronnie? Maybe some womanish sentimentality, he might think, a gift to the church, a few dollars to a favourite student, an ornament to Addy. Nothing she couldn't tell them, and they would look after it without a will. But he couldn't refuse, though he looked hurt and puzzled.

Already she was framing the conversation with Charlie Groat in her mind. She could hear him ask, "You're sure? You want it all to go to your daughter-in-law? No strings attached? Is it really for the children?"

"No," she would say, "I trust Linda. She'll know what to do with it."

"Well, well, Mrs. Fanjoy," he would say, "you women all think you're better at holding onto the money than the men are. Very steady girl, your daughter-in-law, as you say.

She'll take care of it."

It was all right if that was what Charlie Groat thought, or what the others thought, but what about Linda? She mustn't think that.

Now, with the others leaving, she must have a chance to speak to Linda alone. Call her back. The others will think it's a message for the children.

"Linda?"

"Yes, Mrs. Fanjoy?"

Not Mother Fanjoy this time?

Tell her quickly—she mustn't delay her too long after the others. No time for the luxury of a long scene. "Linda, it's my money."

Linda stood there puzzled, questioning. How was Sophie to go on? Nothing to do but blurt it out. "Look, Linda, there's more than they think, and I'm leaving it to you."

Linda was startled. "To me? Oh, Mrs. Fanjoy, I didn't even think you liked me." She saw she had been too honest, continued hastily, in a determination to be even more honest, Sophie supposed, "I can't take money from you. It wouldn't be right. Leave it to Ronnie. He's your son. To the children even, but not to me."

Sophie was filled with a kind of desperation. Surely her effort was not to be in vain. "Why shouldn't you take it? You came into the family the same way I did. You've had a hard time. I'm not given to throwing my feelings about, but you deserve something."

Now Linda was in tears. "No I don't. Mrs. Fanjoy, you have to understand. I'd like to leave Ronnie. If it weren't for the children I would. When they grow up I think I will. I can't take your money when I don't love your son." There, it was out, she seemed to be saying.

But if Linda could be honest, so could Sophie. "I don't love him much either," she said.

There, that startled the girl.

"Why shouldn't you take it?" she continued. "Don't you see? I'm not giving you the money to tie you to him. I'm giving it to you to free you if you want to be free."

A silence. A touch on her hand. Then Linda said, "Do what you want, Mother. Do what you want. I don't know if one person can free another, but thank you for trying."

Linda's kiss on her forehead. Sophie was tired. And she would have to nod and smile at dear deaf Mrs. Harris, now that the others had all gone. But she had won.

"A beautiful family," Mrs. Harris said, "you have such a beautiful family, Mrs. Fanjoy. Almost as beautiful as mine." And she nodded in the direction of her imaginary son and daughter, sitting on the chairs by her bed.

Tomorrow, maybe, Charlie Groat would be here. And she would do what she could to set Linda free. From one trap to another? But it was up to Linda what she did with the money. She wasn't compelling Linda to leave. For all she knew, Linda might just buy new furniture. No, she was only giving her a choice. To leave or to stay. Wasn't it always good to have a choice, as she hadn't had? Arguing with herself was more trouble than arguing with her daughter-in-law.

After she had done what she could for Linda, she also would be free. But not to stay.

Suppose she didn't wake up in the morning, or was too deathly sick to see Charlie Groat? Suppose she took a sudden turn for the worse with that new chemotherapy treatment?

No, of course she would wake up. Of course she would feel only a little worse. The other would be too easy on her. It wouldn't happen that way.

COMFORT ME WITH APPLES

Helen, having decided to kill herself, thought she could afford a better lunch than she would otherwise have done. There was no point drowning herself on an empty stomach. She might as well go to the university cafeteria rather than to Joe's place, which was cheaper but greasier. Office salaries, in these postwar days, were not keeping up with expenses, and she was usually very cautious about money. But today she did not need to be.

The big, rather shabby room was just filling up. Students and office workers like Helen lined up with trays, and there was a clattering of crockery and cutlery as the line moved sluggishly past the kitchen help who were dishing up food. Helen took a bowl of soup, a salad, and a slab of rather heavy-looking raisin pie. Paying the girl at the turnstile, she wondered if she was leaving enough to pay for supper, and then remembered that she did not need to worry about supper. She would not be here for it.

She found an empty table in the corner of the room, set down the tray, and put her handbag on the floor by her chair. Seated, she looked around. She did not know any of the faces. She looked at them with a feeling of complete detachment, as though they belonged to another race. Did any of them, she wondered, feel at all the same way she did? Could any of them look at her and guess how she felt? But obviously she did not create any particular impression of misery. The blond boy reading a book which he had leaned against a ketchup bottle, the fat girl in a sweater too tight for her, had glanced at her for a minute when she came in and then had turned their eyes away again. She did not imagine she looked as if she planned to kill herself. Her hair was tidily combed. She had put on lipstick and her best suit and a blue nylon blouse. She knew there were no tears on her face because she had not been able to cry.

If she could only cry perhaps she would be all right. Or if she could talk to someone. But she felt absolutely wooden, or maybe more like cork, as though if somebody stuck pins in her she wouldn't feel it. Her stomach felt queasy, as if she were just about to write an examination which she was sure she would fail. She didn't want the soup, but after all she had paid for it and ought to eat it. "Think of all the poor children who would be glad. . ." her mother's voice seemed to echo in her ears.

It was on Saturday morning at work that she had got the letter telling her that Andrew and Margaret were married.

She had not opened the letter in the cataloguing department of the library, where she had started to work as a typist last month. She had opened it in the empty staff room, just before going home after the morning's work, and for a few minutes had felt rather proud of herself because she hadn't felt like crying. And then she had suddenly felt cold and started to tremble violently, and afterward she had been sick to her stomach in the women's washroom. Miss Purvis had come in while she was washing her face afterward and they had talked about the weather. For a minute she had almost thought of saying, "Miss Purvis, I'm very unhappy," but after all, how could she? She didn't know Miss Purvis. Besides, Miss Purvis always stood perfectly straight and the seams of her stockings were always perfectly straight.

Saturday afternoon she had gone downtown and picked out a wedding present for Andrew and Margaret. One was supposed to be cheerful and not jealous. She wished she could have sent them something more extravagant, to show how cheerful she felt, but of course that was another one of the troubles. She did not really make enough at the job to live on. She had to add up the amount she spent on meals very carefully every day or else she might run out of money for food before the end of the month.

People with enough money, she thought, don't die of broken hearts. Or loneliness, or fear, or whatever it was she felt like dying of. People with money go off on expensive trips. They buy expensive clothes and have their hair done. They don't have to go to work when they don't feel like it. They can phone their families long distance when they are in a strange town and have no-one to talk to.

On Sunday afternoon she had gone walking by the lake. She always liked to walk by water. Shouldn't looking at something so beautiful make her happy? But she felt so tired, so drained of life. If only she could lie down at the bottom of all that water, with the weight of it pressing on her eyes.

In the evening she had gone to church. She had not much believed in God since high school, but she liked to go sometimes because she thought the prayers beautiful. But beautiful prayers, she decided, weren't much more helpful than beautiful scenery if you didn't believe in them. Kneeling in her place she prayed desperately, "Oh God, I don't believe in you. If you are real, make me believe." But it was no use. She could not believe. Life would go on being deadly for years, and then she would die and there would be an end of it. Or maybe religion was true, but she couldn't feel it to be true, and if you didn't feel it to be true, what did its truth matter?

Perhaps, she wondered, she might stop and talk to the minister. But she knew that talking to him wouldn't be sensible. She didn't know him any more than she knew Miss Purvis, and it was easy enough to see that he had never been miserable.

In her room that night, when she could not sleep, she had turned on the light again and picked up the book on her bedside table. It was a novel by a young man who, she had read somewhere, drowned himself. She wondered how he had felt before he drowned. Her cousin Rose nearly drowned once by accident. She had told Helen about it, how she had felt awful at first, and then how beautiful and pleasant a dream she had seemed to be having, and then how painful the recovery had been. "But it would be an easy death," she had said. Helen turned out the light again and thought of death lapping over her in soft waves.

And now she was sitting here in the cafeteria finishing her lunch. In the afternoon she was supposed to go to one of the other offices and help address envelopes for the college magazine with the addressograph. She had never used the machine before. Now she would never know how. Because she was too tired to go on working. If she could get on the train and travel for miles and miles maybe she might be all right. Even if she could go home and lie down and sleep she might be all right. But she had to go to work. She had no vacation or sick leave coming. She had almost no money. The only way she could get a rest was to die.

From the cafeteria she walked back to her room. It was not a bad room; as a matter of fact it was rather pleasant, and perhaps that was why she didn't have enough money for lunch. It was small and clean, with walls that were a little too pink. She combed her hair in front of the mirror and put on some fresh lipstick. No, she would not leave a note. People who left notes said such silly things. She walked softly down the stairs again, avoiding her landlady, Mrs. Peacock, and Mrs. Peacock's daughter Anne, who was rattling dishes in the kitchen.

She made her way, almost automatically, along the streets that led to the lake. There was a long walk running by the water, with green benches on the grass, now all deserted on this dark autumnal day. The water lay grey and sullen and restless in front of her. At intervals stone steps led down to it, with metal handrails at each side. Looking at the waves, Helen felt her stomach tighten, and was sorry she had eaten lunch first. There was still time, after all, to go back to work. Perhaps she would feel better at work. But she knew she would not.

She walked back and forth along the shore for a while, with a sense of walking in a dream. A man came by, and she had to wait till he was past. Now, she thought, the time had gone for returning to work. She would have to explain her absence. She did not know how. She took her wrist watch off and put it in her handbag. Then she laid the handbag on one of the benches and walked over to the steps.

For a long time she stood at the foot of the flight of stone steps making up her mind, and then, with a sense of release, almost with a sense of triumph, she stepped off into the water and waded away from the shore.

She had hardly walked more than half a dozen steps when she realized how silly she would look to anyone watching from shore. But fortunately nobody was watching. She must walk out as fast as she could beyond her depth. Then, as she did not know how to swim, she would not have a choice any longer.

But it was remarkable how long she took getting beyond her depth. The iciness of the water and the tangles of coarse grass which floated in it seemed to wake her from the dream in which she had previously been moving. The water no longer looked restful. It tugged heavily at her skirt, and she thought what a shame it was to ruin her one good suit. And then she stepped off a shelf into deep water and was over her head.

Involuntarily, in spite of all her intentions, she found herself struggling. Slimy green water pressed into her nose and mouth, and she gulped it down. "I must let myself drown," she thought. "That's what I wanted." But fear came over her, the fear of her body struggling with death. She thought of how her mother and father and her younger brother would feel, and how they would talk about her, and wonder why she had drowned herself. And she remembered going to church with her family and listening to old Canon Thomas, who preached such dull sermons. Then God, whom she could not believe in the night before, seemed to be with her, a presence infinitely loving, beautiful and sad. She felt the spirit of life protesting against her throwing life away.

She struggled to save herself, but seemed to be farther from shore. There was nobody in sight to call. She was too tired to try any longer. "I can't," she prayed, or almost prayed. "I can't do any more." And she closed her eyes and let herself go limp.

Then, to her surprise, the water seemed to lift her up, and she floated. She almost laughed aloud. Because when her brother had tried to teach her to float by going limp she had never in the world been able to do it. And now, somehow, she managed to find her way back to the shelf of firm ground and from there to walk slowly to shore.

When she reached the top of the steps again, she paused, wondering what to do. She was thankful, after all, not to be dead, but how could she walk home in her wet clothes along these streets? As she stood leaning on the rail wringing the water out of her hair, a man came by and looked at her. She realized by his stare of distaste how strange her appearance must be.

"What have you been doing?" he asked.

"I was trying to kill myself but decided not to," Helen answered. Her voice, she noticed, sounded distant and a little blurred.

"You would probably have been more sensible to finish the job," the man said coldly, and turned and walked in the other direction. She saw him disappearing like a figure in a dream.

Helen decided she must walk home. Perhaps she might be lucky and not meet anyone else. She found her handbag where she had left it on the bench by the water. She managed to get through the park without being seen. But then there were all those streets. And supposing Mrs. Peacock met her at the door. How could she explain her dripping clothes? She began to shiver, feeling their sogginess. Perhaps the man was right. She would go back to the lake again.

Then she saw that a man was coming in her direction

from the garden of one of the houses. He was a tall, erect, white-headed man in shirt sleeves. He walked straight toward her with his hand outstretched and said, "I don't think we've met, but I'm a neighbour of yours. Colonel Allen."

"What an odd man," Helen thought.

"My wife would like to see you," he continued. "Won't you come in?"

In the midst of her sense of dream, she found herself guided up the walk and into a hall, and then into a kitchen where a big, red-faced, motherly woman was pouring tea. She put her arms around Helen and said, speaking with a hint of a brogue, "Oh, the poor little girl." And then Helen began to cry. She sat down at the kitchen table and leaned her head on the table; and tears poured out of her eyes as though the lake were filling them. "There, there," the woman said. "It's all over."

But that was why she was able to cry, because it was all over.

In the hospital she lay in a half dream in the white, antiseptic room. She was too tired to worry about the future or regret the past. When she closed her eyes brilliant figures danced in front of them, strings of coloured lights, Christmas trees, flowering plants of technicolour brilliance.

There had been all sorts of people. There had been a policeman who had promised that her family wouldn't know anything about it. There had been a doctor who had given her pills and another one who said he shouldn't have given her pills. There had been the university chaplain, who had said the head librarian must know, but other people needn't. She was glad Miss Purvis wouldn't know.

Those had been the real people.

Then, when she closed her eyes, there were other people: her parents, Canon Thomas, the man who had told her she should have finished the job. Especially there were Andrew and Margaret. They would not seem to go away. They stood by her bed, wearing raincoats, and water seemed to pour over them. They were holding hands. Margaret was wearing a bandanna. Andrew's head was bare, and Helen could see drops of rain running down his forehead. Sometimes she was glad they were beside her. They were almost a comfort. Other times she wished they would go away. Finally they disappeared, and she watched instead fireworks falling over water.

In the middle of the night she awoke, sick to her stomach. The nauseous green water came up, and her undigested lunch. She was too weak to get to the bathroom and too slow in ringing the bell for the nurse, so that the slime poured out over her pillow. Someone cool and starched remade her bed and washed her face, and she went to sleep again.

The next day the second doctor, the one who had said she ought not to have had pills, came in. He talked to her about another girl who had taken an overdose of sleeping pills, but who now, so he said, was quite well and happy. Helen tried hard to listen to him, but couldn't manage to very well. He went away, and she slept, and woke, and tried to eat some dinner but could not. He came in again, and talked to her about the cottage where he went fishing on weekends. "Sometimes," he said, "I don't think I could stand life if I couldn't go fishing. Not so much for the fish, I mean, as for sitting looking at the water. Is there anything like fishing that you do?"

"Not fishing," she answered, and smiled without expecting to. "I don't think I could bear looking at the water just now."

"I don't think I'd avoid it," he said gravely.

"I feel a coward," she told him. "As if I couldn't bear either to live or to die."

"More people are like that than you think. None of us knows how we'd take bad news at a bad time. You mustn't think you're alone." Then he said, "You're tired. You'd better go to sleep again."

The lights no longer shone in front of her eyes in the darkness. She slept wearily, almost dreamlessly, and awoke with only a slight ache in the back of her head. Blue autumn weather, bright and frosty, shone outside her window. She could still not manage to eat much breakfast, but lay and drowsed in the sunshine.

In the afternoon, while she was still drowsing, the door opened gently and a slight, fair girl came in. It was her landlady's daughter, Anne Peacock. Helen had hardly ever seen her, and they hadn't had much to say to each other.

"It's lovely out for a walk," Anne said. "The leaves are so red in the park. You must go for a walk when you're over your 'flu."

Helen thought, "I must try and think about her. She is another person. She's a few years younger than I am, but not much. She has her own life." She added up in her mind the fair hair, the blue eyes, the pink cheeks, the green blazer, the plaid skirt, the brown loafers.

"Are they burning the leaves?" she asked. "I thought I smelled leaves burning."

Anne put a brown paper bag on the bed. "Apples," she said. "I thought you might like some."

They were polished and perfect, gold streaked with rich ripe red. Their fragrance, sweet but with a delicate hint of sharpness, subdued the antiseptic smell of the hospital room. They seemed to bring the autumn world that lay outside the window into the room and hold it wrapped inside their thin, clear skin. Helen took one out of the bag and laid it on the coverlet to admire.

When Anne had left, Helen felt hungry for the first time

since she had been in the hospital. She picked up the apple, turned it over in her hands, and at last bit into it. The white flesh, streaked with pink veins, tasted of outdoors. She ate it all, down to the core, and lay holding the tiny remnant with its brown seeds inside it cupped gently in her hand.

IT'S EASY TO FALL ON THE ICE

Margaret awoke while it was still dark, before the alarm went off, hearing the little boy in the apartment above her bounce his ball on the floor. Peering at the luminous dial of the clock on her bedside table, she saw that the time was a quarter to seven, and pressed the little button before the alarm could go off. She lay on her back for a few minutes, stretching her arms above her head and groaning a little bit at the prospect of facing a new day and a new week. Her mind dived back into her dreams, in which she had been talking about vacations to Rosemary Harvey, James Harvey's daughter. The weather in her dream had been warm summer weather, and they had been sitting outdoors in the Harveys' back yard. "And are you going somewhere exciting on your vacation?" she had been asking the girl with a faint touch of amused motherliness in her tone. And Rosemary had answered, "Oh, yes, really exciting. We're going to the moon."

"To the moon! All the family? Oh, I do envy you."

And as she awoke she was thinking, "I wonder if people really do go to the moon on vacations now. I must find out."

And then she was fully awake, in the dark February morning, to a world where there were no vacations on the moon. Maybe that space travel affair at Expo.

She threw off the covers, turned on the bedside lamp, and got up to close the window. At least it was not storming or anything. How she hated getting up in the morning, especially on Monday morning, after being spoiled by the weekend.

After her quick, lukewarm bath and a few halfhearted exercises she felt more nearly awake and kinder toward the world. Her weight, she was pleased to see, stayed steady at 113 pounds. Her figure, she thought, was not bad, after all, for a woman of thirty-nine, though she had to be careful about her hips. There were fine lines here and there, around her eyes and mouth, but her skin was still young, and she remembered her mother, apple-cheeked in old age. Her hair, of course. It had begun to go grey early, and she hated the thought of dyeing it. And this morning there was no wave in it. It really depressed her. But she was going to the hairdresser on her way home. At least she would have a set.

What should she put on? The green dress, which her niece Ursula had turned up for her? No, it had just been dry-cleaned, and the workmen were still tearing up the building. Something not too good. Her old blue skirt and sweater and the red cardigan. A cheerful colour, anyhow.

In the kitchen, with an apron on over the blue skirt, she put the kettle on, took out of the fridge the other half of yesterday morning's grapefruit, wrapped in plastic. It didn't taste as fresh as yesterday morning, but after all it was still good. Corn Flakes. She sat at her kitchen table eating them and watching the lights in the kitchen window across the street. Brown toast and tea. She kept the country custom of tea for breakfast rather than coffee. Soothing drink, lulling to the nerves. You needed to be soothed when listening to the morning news. She turned on the radio. Constitutional conference at Ottawa. Vietnam as usual, maybe a little worse. Fire in Woodstock. By this time she was back in the bathroom cleaning her teeth. Then the weather. A little colder with possible snow flurries. She put on her warm red hat, which she liked, her red scarf, her rather shabby seal coat, her snow boots.

Yesterday had been sunny and almost like spring after Saturday's rain. This morning was a little colder. An icy morning, with the bumpy snow covered by a crust of ice. Margaret usually liked walking to work, but not on icy mornings. She was always afraid of falling. Another of her dreams popped up in her mind. In her dream she and the head librarian, Mr. Titus, had been housecleaning an attic full of books. That was all right, but in the midst of the dream she had had to come down from the attic on a ladder, and the ladder had not quite touched the floor. It had swung a little as she came down, and she had been giddy and afraid of falling.

There was always difficulty getting across the street just at this place at this hour. Cars were coming in both directions, some on their way up to the university, some bound, as she was, for government offices downtown. Dodging across in a break in the traffic, she wished, as usual, that someone had put lights at the corner. Only she wanted to cross before the corner to mail her letters. Nothing exciting, only the cheque for her telephone bill and another cheque to a church Save-a-Family plan which was supposed to help some family in India. She tried to imagine India, but could think only of a blur of heat and flies, perhaps some mud huts, women in saris with red dots on their foreheads, a few hungry-looking children.

She had turned the corner, was walking along Charlotte Street past the florist's shop. Two little girls, on their way to school, passed her and ran ahead. "How sure they are on the ice," Margaret thought enviously. Then one of them, the smaller one, sat down suddenly. But she was not hurt. She jumped up, looked around to make sure she was not being laughed at, then dusted herself off and went on with a little shake.

Church Street next. Even on a rather ugly day, this was a beautiful town, Margaret thought. The Victorian Gothic houses would have been ugly in stone, but in wood, painted white or green or sometimes pink, they had a bright, fly-away look which she liked. She met a few students on foot, a young man with long hair and a beard, some girls in slacks or in short skirts with long woollen stockings and high boots. Curious how they looked alike. She remembered that when she was in her teens herself she thought that women in their forties and fifties all looked alike. Now it was the young girls. The reason people used to say "All Chinese look alike," or whatever it was. Do cats look very different and individual to cats? At least, cats of one's own acquaintance, age group, social circle?

She came within sight of the Cathedral, but did not pass it. Also Victorian Gothic, but nice. A replica, supposedly, of a parish church in England. In summer, when the lawn was green, one could prowl around Bishop Medley's tomb in the churchyard, and imagine oneself in an English village, especially if one was not very well acquainted with English villages. Margaret knew more about the Bishop under the tomb than about the present Bishop. She had read in the library where she worked his pastoral charges, his speech when the Cathedral had been opened, the funeral sermon on his son's death, descriptions of his wife.

It was 8.25 when she reached the Legislative Building and entered the side door which was nearest to her office. The men had finally finished laying the new tile floor in the hall, a dark rose which looked, she thought, rather suited to a kitchen. It was covered with dust and rubble. Picking her way through the rubble, she unlocked the door, first of her own office, then of the main library. Hanging up her coat in her office, she ran a comb through her hair, tucked her handbag into the bottom drawer of the filing cabinet, and went into the main library, where she turned on the lights. Another Victorian room. Heavy old bookcases, ornate chairs, a grandfather clock which chimed the hours and the quarters. But a pleasant room, sunny and cheerful, although somewhat too crowded with books and furniture and flags and royal pictures. Most of the time it was shining and free from dust because Mr. Titus hated dust, but now even here a faint grey film had penetrated, though not so much as in the rest of the building. And as she thought of Mr. Titus he came in, unlocking the door on the other side of the room, brisk and tidy as usual. He was followed by young Eddie Doucet, still yawning.

"God, another messy day here," Eddie said. "What they want to fix this old place up for, when they might as well tear it down and build new."

"Now Eddie, a beautiful old place like this," Mr. Titus protested. "Margaret, can you persuade Eddie this is a beautiful old place?"

"Yes, a beautiful old place, but crowded."

"A dump," Eddie said decisively, "a dump."

So they could discuss their space problem for ten minutes. Libraries always have space problems, Margaret reflected.

By the time she was back in her office Marlene was there, late as usual. Marlene was her typist, tall, blonde, buxom. She had a rich, milk-fed figure, but every now and then thought she would like to look like the most slender of models and went on a diet of eggs and grapefruit. "Guess how much I lost this weekend, Miss Estabrook," she said. "Ten pounds. Ten whole pounds. Don't I look thinner? Gosh, this place is going to be dusty again. Do you know, Andrew and I broke up this weekend?"

"Oh, I thought you broke up last weekend."

"We did, but we made up again. But then I met this new man, see, and Andrew, you know how jealous he is, well the thing is. . ."

Margaret picked up a book and waited for Marlene's voice to run down. New Brunswick collection books to catalogue. This one gave information to intending settlers back in the eighteen-twenties. And there were those speeches of Sir George Foster, impassioned pleas for the Empire. Well, people didn't write impassioned pleas for the Empire any longer. Funny, even when she was a child at school, the Empire was still a great thing. You were proud of being a British Subject, and looked up all the red bits on the map of the world. But then the War had changed all that.

She would have to try to find the dates of the man who wrote the book for intending settlers. And the name of the man who wrote this anonymous description of the cholera epidemic in Saint John, brought in by some of those settlers.

Mr. Titus came in. "What would you do with this thing, anyway?" he asked. "Would you call it a folder? And it's in French and English, but the French isn't a translation of the

English. If I describe it as in French and English won't that sound as if the text were the same in both languages?" He sat down. "There are always these great problems." He ran his fingers over the edge of the book truck and looked sadly at the dust on his fingers. "All this dirt and noise."

At ten, with Mr. Titus back in his office, Marlene jumped up from her desk and started to put on her coat. "Coffee for you, Miss Estabrook? I guess I'll get some. Don't you want this door closed? All that pounding outside."

The room to herself for a few minutes. She got up and looked out the window. She could see Marlene walking across the street to the pizza place on the corner. Marlene slipped on a patch of ice, steadied herself. A flight to the moon, Margaret thought. That would be a vacation.

The coffee stayed moderately warm in its container. "Would you like a doughnut?" Marlene asked. " I bought two."

"Not doughnuts, Marlene. I thought you were dieting."

"That was last weekend. I just lost ten pounds. Anyhow, I feel bad about Andrew, so I have to eat. I like this new man, but I'm sort of used to Andrew, see. Funny how you get used to someone."

She bit into the doughnut with satisfaction.

"You know what that woman in that little place told me," she said. "Well, you know they said Mr. Berryman broke his leg falling on the ice? Well, she says he didn't fall on the ice. His brother-in-law—that's his wife's brother—threw him downstairs because he was flirting with his wife. The brother-in-law's wife, that is. She knows because she has a cousin lives near the brother-in-law in Moncton. Isn't that awful? Incest, practically, isn't it? And for a man in his position, too. Don't you think?"

"I don't know. It's easy to fall on the ice this time of year."

"Oh, well. I thought it was interesting. Look, there's a

whole bunch of cards for you to check, Miss Estabrook. I typed a lot Friday."

Marlene was a good typist. There were not too many mistakes on the cards, but checking them was a dull job, and Margaret supposed typing them was a dull job too. No wonder there were mistakes sometimes. The cards swam before her eyes and ran into each other.

"Have they still got the hall to the Ladies' blocked off, Marlene?" she asked.

"Yes. The easiest place to go now is that washroom upstairs. You know, you go up the back stairs and through on the other side of the Visitors' Gallery."

Up the back stairs, past empty committee rooms, through a door leading into the Gallery, looking down into the Assembly Chamber beneath. Even the Assembly Chamber was messy. The carpet had been covered, most of the chairs huddled into a corner. The portraits of George III and Queen Charlotte had been removed from the walls, and the chair from which the Governor read his speeches had been covered with plastic.

Looking down from a height always bothered Margaret. She supposed she was afraid of falling. She was glad when she had got to the other side, through another door, and into the washroom. One spent so much time visiting bathrooms, it was a waste, especially when you had to walk this distance. She needed a little fresh lipstick.

Today was payday, and Eddie brought the cheques over from the Centennial Building. "It's started to snow," he said, shaking himself as he came in. "Makes it treacherous out."

"Money. Good," Marlene said. "I think I'll buy a snowsuit for my niece. She's getting real cute now. Real little mischief. Walks all over the place. Did I show you her picture?"

There was time, after cashing the cheque at noon, to run into Sally's Style Shop and pick up the pink dressing gown she had been looking at. Now it was snowing quite hard, and a cold February wind was blowing. Shoppers hurried along the street with coat collars turned up, slipping now and then.

She decided to eat at the hotel, and found a table beside a window where she could look out at the frozen river with the snow falling on it. She ordered hot soup, because it was cold outside, and a fruit salad because fruit salad made her think of summer. Chunks of pear slipped icily down her throat. It was a pity they had done up the dining-room in this very summery style for Centennial year. It had suited the feel of summer; but summer was so short, and now it looked cold. Hot coffee gave her a drowsy, peaceful feeling. I wonder if James is back from Ottawa, she thought.

Marlene rushed into the office, her arms full of parcels. "They have a shoe sale on at Killeens," she said, "and I just couldn't afford not to get two pairs. And what do you think of this blue dress? I have to take it up, but otherwise it fits me perfect. And the snowsuit for Nancy. And you know those big stuffed animals? Zellers had a sale, and you know she just loves them. I didn't have time to eat. It's a good job I had those doughnuts."

Marlene was filing in the library catalogue. Margaret picked up a few of the new books. The one by Trudeau. Bertrand Russell's *Autobiography*. The book by Lloyd George's widow.

Later, when Marlene came in, she went out and checked the filing. Eddie was opening parcels of government documents. "I don't know why I stay on this job," he said. "Why do you?"

"I don't know. There are worse places. I like the town. I

have friends."

"Oh, friends. You can always get those. What I want is money."

Marlene's filing was not as good as her typing. Margaret shook her head to keep awake.

Marlene came out. "I brought your coffee, Miss Estabrook. Have you seen the paper? Isn't the news awful, as usual? Eddie, did I tell you what I heard about Mr. Berryman? Oh, you heard it already?"

Back in the office, Margaret drank the coffee. Marlene was having Coke this time. "I wonder if Eddie's wife is mean to him," she said. "Sometimes he's that grumpy, and a man usually has a reason. Oh, did I tell you what the cleaning woman told me? That she saw Pete Hughes kissing Mrs. Pridham in the hall? Mrs. Pridham must be twenty years older than Pete Hughes and he has that beautiful wife and three little children. I think it's a sin, don't you?"

The phone on Margaret's desk rang. "It's for you," she said to Marlene, and got up to do some more checking.

"That was Andrew," Marlene told her when she came back. "I'm glad I bought that blue dress. Blue is Andrew's favourite colour. He says it matches my eyes. He's very sorry, and we're going to the movies."

The beauty parlour was up a flight of stairs. The steamy smell of damp hair, hair spray and cologne drifted down the stairs to meet Margaret on her way up. There was a fat woman having her hair dyed red, and a girl in her teens having grey streaks put in. Margaret leaned back with pleasure while the warm scented water flowed over her hair and the girl kneaded her scalp.

"You work for the Government, don't you?" the girl asked. "Have you heard what they say about Berryman?"

Sitting under the dryer, Margaret picked up the paper. Dismal, as Marlene said. Mrs. Berryman's picture, taken at a tea, on the women's page. Before or after her husband's broken leg? Not a pretty woman, she decided.

The snow made the walk home cleaner and brighter, though dusk had come on by the time she reached the apartment building. No mail except a couple of magazines and a letter from her sister in New Glasgow. She opened the letter while she cooked her steak. Nothing new. Fred and the children had colds. Fanny was busy with women's groups. She must get down for a long weekend some time. She felt depressed suddenly, got up and clattered the dishes vigorously as she washed them.

She would put on the new pink dressing gown and have another cup of coffee while she watched television.

She had almost fallen asleep, sitting in the big leather chair, when the phone rang.

"Peggy?" the voice on the other end of the line asked. "Are you busy?"

"No, I'm sitting in my dressing gown falling asleep. When did you get back? Where are you calling from?"

"Late this afternoon. From my office. I wanted to catch up on my mail. I thought I'd come over if you weren't busy."

"Yes, of course. What was Ottawa like?"

"Dull. Very dull. I'll be there in ten minutes."

Going into her bedroom she inspected her new hair-do, decided it didn't need combing, hesitated a minute before taking off the dressing gown and slipping into a dress. The blue dress that buttoned up the front, so she didn't have to disturb her hair. After all, Marlene wasn't the only one who had blue eyes.

James was at the door already. "I thought I was going to see you in the new dressing gown," he said. "Are you tired? You sounded tired on the phone."

"No, just drowsy. Would you like some sherry? Ottawa was dull?"

"Moderately dull. Did you miss me?"

"I always miss you." She handed him the sherry and sat down beside him on the living-room chesterfield.

"What did you do today? What happened in Fredericton?"

"Nothing happened. I nearly fell on the ice, but I didn't quite manage to."

"Poor Peggy," he said, putting down the glass. "You didn't even manage to fall."

Drawing her to him, he began to stroke her breasts. She relaxed and closed her eyes, leaning her head on his shoulder.

"I hear Alan Berryman fell," he said. "Did you hear anything about that?"

SILENT MOVIE

The plane trip, in spite of Mrs. Simpson's initial nervousness, had been uneventful and peaceful enough. She sat between a young girl who was reading a glossy magazine and a middle-aged man, perhaps her own age, who was reading what looked to be a detective story. None of them spoke to each other all night except when one or the other of them got up to go to the washroom. Mrs. Simpson looked at a French phrase-book and a guidebook to Paris. After dinner there was a movie, but the earphones she rented didn't work. The movie was set sometime in the twenties, and, in the absence of sound, might almost have been made at that time. Mrs. Simpson amused herself for a while trying to follow the story without knowing the words people were saying, but the attempt became rather a strain, and she closed her eyes.

It was almost impossible to sleep, she thought, in such a cramped position, but in fact she did for an hour or so, and awoke with a pain, literally a pain in her neck. When she looked around, almost all the passengers were asleep. There was something frightening in the sight of all these unconscious people, wedged so tightly together and hurtling through space. Thank goodness the night was short. Six hours of it lost by the change in time between Toronto and Paris.

In the morning she washed her face, swallowed the rolls and bitter coffee brought by the stewardess. The voice on the loudspeaker announced when they were passing England, and she wished for a moment that she was coming down in London instead of Paris. She knew London, had visited it with Roy, her husband, when he was alive. And in London people spoke English.

She busied herself again with the phrase-book. It was not reassuring. The tourist, it seemed, must be prepared for all sorts of difficulties. Just look at the English side of the book: "I don't understand you.—What is the matter?—I cannot speak French.—Where are we going?—My bag has been stolen.—That man is following me everywhere. I shall call a policeman.—Help! Fire! Thief!—Beware of. . . Who are you?—Leave me alone.—I did not know the rules.—I have already paid you.—Where is the British Consulate?" And then there were the visits to the dentist and the doctor. But no doubt he (more likely she?) was all right as soon as he found the British Consulate.

A safe, smooth, efficient landing at Charles de Gaulle

airport. A rapid whisking through customs and immigration. No lost luggage. It was all too easy. She had better take a taxi rather than try a public transport. Her French was just not good enough.

She handed the taxi driver the address of her hotel. No problem. She leaned back and watched the approach of the strange city.

But the traffic. It was worse than Montreal. They were surrounded by other cars, by big trucks. She would have liked to speak to her driver, to make some comment on the traffic, but she could not think of words. They were right behind a really huge lorry. Wasn't it too near? Suddenly she felt a jolt, was thrown partly forward, bruising her lip against the seat in front of her.

Her driver and the driver of the truck got out and confronted each other. They seemed to be arguing, or were they merely consulting? One or two passers-by also stopped and talked. Mrs. Simpson watched them apprehensively from inside the taxi. Finally her driver opened the back door of the taxi and gestured to her to get out. Was she being abandoned to find another taxi in the midst of this strange city? However, he led her, carrying her two suitcases, to a spot where he hailed another taxi.

The second taxi driver was young, an Oriental—Chinese, perhaps?—in sunglasses. He had a stolid air which was reassuring. Perhaps he would deliver her to her hotel without accident. She would have liked to talk to him about the accident—at home, in Regina, she liked to be friendly to taxi drivers and waiters and clerks in stores—but did not know if he could speak English. She contented herself with handing him the address of her hotel, and then turned her attention with curiosity to the streets of the strange city.

It was May, a bright morning, hot but not too hot. Crowds of people were out, some on the sidewalks, many in cars. Mrs. Simpson was relieved that she could read most of the signs in shop windows. It was the thought of framing a sentence in French that alarmed her. But there were so many streets. Were they going on forever? Would she have enough money in francs to pay for the taxi? She clutched her purse nervously.

She wished Roy was with her. He had always managed things, was competent with money and languages. But, she reminded herself, she would only be alone for a day or two. Her brother and sister-in-law were meeting her, and after that they would take the train to Rouen together and she would be travelling with them.

She had not observed the turn into the rue Vaneau, and was surprised when they stopped. This was her hotel. A small hotel that a friend had recommended. The girl at the desk was slender and neat, dressed quietly and unfashionably. Mrs. Simpson approved. She spoke English (Mrs. Simpson was relieved to discover) in a careful, rather schoolgirlish way. Mrs. Simpson signed the register, and soon found herself and her suitcases packed into a tiny elevator on her way up to her room. The elevator was an ancient contraption, a sort of cage that was raised or lowered with what looked like ropes. Mrs. Simpson looked at it with distrust and was thankful she had not let herself become too fat.

"English? From Angleterre?" the maid who was helping her with her luggage asked.

"Canadienne," Mrs. Simpson answered, but could go no further.

"Montréal?" the woman asked, obviously delighted.

"Regina, Saskatchewan," Mrs. Simpson answered, and was not surprised by the blank look she received in return. She would probably have been given that look in Montreal.

She was cheered by her room, rather an old-fashioned room, she thought; very feminine, with a scrolled and flowered wallpaper in pale blue, a fat pink bed, and pink curtains. No TV, of course. Looking out into the street from her window, she could see people sitting at little tables in front of a combined shop and café. The roll and coffee she had had for breakfast had been digested a long time ago. She needed something more.

Half an hour later she also was sitting down at one of the little tables. Because there was no printed menu to point to, she had some trouble ordering, but a cheese sandwich and coffee would at least keep body and soul together. Wine would have seemed more suitable to Paris than coffee, she thought, but she was not sure what kind to ask for, and in any event felt light-headed enough already.

Again she wished for Roy. He would have known how to order a decent meal. Even if he hadn't, they would have enjoyed their cheese-filled rolls together, lazily watching the passers-by, inventing stories about them. It was a pity they had never managed the trip during his lifetime. He would have enjoyed it so much. By herself, she could not linger here in the afternoon sun as she would have done with him. She wanted someone to whom she was Caroline, not Mrs. Simpson.

After lunch, she was too tired to explore the neighbourhood. Returning to her room, she undressed, soaked herself in the pink tub in the bathroom, and blotted herself dry on one of the large white towels. "Imagine a bathroom with stained glass windows," she thought. "It's like bathing in church." Roy would have been amused.

Curling up in the centre of the fat pink bed, she lay luxuriously waiting for sleep. There must be a school nearby. She heard the voices of boys and girls in their playground, calling out to one another. "The voices of children everywhere are the same," she thought. "But no, that's not true. These voices are higher, more birdlike, than the voices of the children in Regina." She couldn't tell what they were saying.

That was Tuesday. Ted and Ruby were to arrive, she thought, on Wednesday—on Thursday at the latest.

Wednesday morning she ate breakfast in the tiny restaurant of the hotel. She longed vainly for bacon and eggs, and hungrily drank all the milk that came with her breakfast coffee. She went for a walk after breakfast, but didn't want to go too far from the hotel for fear Ted or Ruby would telephone. She would delay her sightseeing for their arrival. The weather was cloudy, not as pleasant as yesterday; but she enjoyed the signs of spring in the city, the lilacs and flowering chestnut. She bought a newspaper to read with her lunch, checking the unfamiliar words with the little dictionary she carried in her purse. She envisaged herself as a seasoned traveller, sitting reading her copy of *Le Figaro* while she waited for her coq au vin (here there was a menu, thank goodness). Her eye was caught by a heading in the newspaper, *Demain journée d'action CGT—CFDT*, with a sub-heading, *Trains, courrier, électricité et* TV*: principaux secteurs touchés*. What was a *journée d'action*? In the story below the heading, the words *grèves* and *arrêts de travail* kept recurring. What was *une grève*? It was not too difficult to guess, but she checked the little dictionary to make sure. Yes—a strike. This looked as if it could be quite a big strike, with electricity, mail, radio and schools possibly affected. And trains. And banks. Would the power be off at her hotel? Would it go off suddenly when she was descending to breakfast in that odd little elevator? Would Ted and Ruby be able to reach Paris? Would they be able to set off for Rouen together by train? And she must find a bank directly after lunch and cash some travellers' cheques. The girl at the desk in the hotel had told her it would be best to cash them at a bank.

She tried to ask her way to a bank; but although she managed to frame the right question, could not manage to understand the answers. But then she always found it hard to follow directions, even in English. The clouds had darkened down, and there was a slight sprinkling of chilly rain. It was the sort of street where one would expect a bank—oh, here was a bank. She had to ring a bell for admission—why was that?—and eventually she managed to cash her cheques. It was really pouring when she came out.

By the time she found her way to the hotel again she was drenched and there was a blister on one of her heels. She inquired at the desk for messages, but there were none. Still no word by dinner time. As the hotel did not serve any meals except breakfast, and she did not want to walk far in the rain with her blistered heel, she contented herself once again with a sandwich in the shop across the street. This time she went inside. There were three or four rough booths at one side of the shop, and she took refuge in one of them with her little dictionary and a guidebook. The young waiter brought the sandwich and cider she ordered. In the booth opposite her a young man and woman were sitting, heads together over their drinks. Mrs. Simpson watched them covertly. She didn't need to know their language to conjecture what was going on between them. And the girl was French, but the man was not. Was he German? No, not German. Scandinavian? They had not many words between them.

She spent most of the evening reading in bed, waiting for the phone to ring. When it had not rung by midnight, she turned off the light and lay on her back, staring at the ceiling, vainly trying to get to sleep. Suppose Ted and Ruby didn't arrive tomorrow, what should she do? Stay here and wait for them? Go on to Rouen by herself? What if that strike really materialized tomorrow? The newspaper had sounded threatening, though vague. If she could talk it over with someone; but there was nobody except the girl at the front desk, whose careful English did not go beyond the most obvious questions and answers. A little better than Mrs. Simpson's French, but not much better.

"It's not soul that makes the difference," Mrs. Simpson argued mentally now with the minister of her church back home in Regina. "It's language that makes us different from the animals. Take away language, and we're animals with no ideas, no sympathies. There's nothing we can ask each other for except the simplest kind of food. Or (she remembered the young man and woman drinking together) the simplest kind of sex." Though of course that wasn't entirely fair. Sex had its own language. She wished Roy was here to speak it with her.

It was hours before she could manage to get to sleep, and even when she did, her sleep was disturbed with bad dreams. In one such dream she was desperately pursuing Roy down the streets of a foreign town, calling out to him in a voice which he did not hear, either because he had become deaf or because she had lost her voice. When she awoke she was making strange grunting sounds, a muffled cry of "Roy! Roy!" Could anyone in the next room have heard her, she wondered? She held her breath and listened for noises on the other side of the wall, but everything was quiet. She got up and took an aspirin, examining her frightened face in the mirror. She wrung out a warm facecloth and applied it to her sticky eyes. Then she went back to bed, burying her face in the pillow.

She was awakened early in the morning by the telephone. It must be Ted or Ruby, she thought, leaping up happily. However, it was only the desk clerk—not the girl, but a man this time—telling her the time. She thanked him and put the receiver back in disappointment. Did he call everybody at seven AM to tell them the time? More likely he had confused her with somebody else who had wanted to be awakened to catch an early train or plane. She considered lifting the receiver to tell him, but decided that the message was too complicated. Probably she would be charged if she phoned down. She would dress and have breakfast early, in case the power went off and there was no hot water.

Hot chocolate this morning, she decided. It was more nourishing than tea or coffee. The little restaurant was full of Germans, a busload of German tourists, very prosperous and substantial. Another language. Half familiar, because she and Roy had had German neighbours when they were first married. Everything seemed cheerful and normal, though she was sleepy after that disturbed night. She would rest after breakfast and wait for her phone call.

It came shortly after ten o'clock. "Ted," she cried delightedly. "When did you arrive? I expected to hear from you yesterday."

"We arrived late last night," Ted told her. "I tried to phone, but your hotel clerk wouldn't put me through. Everything okay?"

"Yes, that is—Ted, do you know anything about a strike? Is the power going to be off? Will the trains be running?"

"Nothing serious, Caroline." (How good to be called Caroline again.) "It's just for the day. We have cold water at our hotel this morning. Some of the trains aren't running, but most of them are. The metro isn't running. Look, why don't you take a taxi to our hotel, and we'll all have lunch together and plan what to do? Ruby wants to shop, and I want to look at the city."

"I'll come right over. You know where I saw you last, Ted? Calgary."

"That's right, Caroline—the Stampede. Great time we had."

And Roy was there too then, she remembered but did not say.

Surprisingly, the taxi driver was the young Chinese who had been her second driver when she arrived. He even recognized her. "American?" he asked when she had given the address of Ted's hotel.

"No, Canadian."

"Canadian? I lived in Canada for two years, in Ottawa. Sometime I go back. It's a good country, Canada—gentle."

Did he mean gentle or *gentil*? A gentle country.

I could have talked to him before, she thought. We speak the same language.

The sun shone brightly on the hurrying crowds and the shops, on a wide avenue, and on a row of chestnut trees. Not a gentle city, but beautiful.

Ted and Ruby were waiting for her in the hotel lobby, so she didn't have to inquire at the desk for them. Ted was a large, slow man; Ruby was short and plump. They moved toward her protectively, Ted loping, Ruby billowing. They were her people. Now she was at home. Now she had someone to talk to.

STRANGERS

I met Hansa Banerji in the fall of 1949. We had both recently arrived in England, she from India, I from Canada. We were both attending King's College, at the University of London, and we were both living in a university hostel in the neighbourhood of Russell Square. My first recollection of her is of meeting her as we set out from the hostel on a morning in early October and discovering that we were on our way to the same place. We were both taking a class in palaeography, where we struggled to make out the crabbed handwriting of medieval or Elizabethan manuscripts in facsimile.

I can't say Hansa made a great impression on me initially, aside from whatever interest I had in the fact that she came from India. She seemed to be plain, polite and middle-aged. In fact, she was around thirty, only seven years older than I was, but I placed her as nearly forty, rather tall and slender, ramrod straight, with wavy brown hair and of course brown eyes. She was wearing an ordinary western blue coat over her sari. Nothing remarkable.

We sat together in the palaeography class. Afterward we went off together to look for the women's washroom. The place, when we found it, was full of a mob of females, mostly rather messy young girls, although one stoutish older woman was standing in front of a mirror applying lipstick. I rushed to one of the cubicles to get rid of all that unaccustomed tea I had drunk at breakfast. At the same time I saw Hansa disappearing into the next cubicle, although I was rather surprised to see her place her handbag on one of the ledges before going in.

She was out before I was, and I heard her startled exclamation as I came out. "My handbag! What happened to my handbag?"

I should have stayed and watched it, I thought. But why?

"Was there much in it?" I asked. "Why did you leave it out like that?"

"Only five pounds. It's not so much the money, but I thought it would be safe."

"Is everybody honest in India, then?" I asked, surprised. And five pounds, I thought, was a lot of money. Would be for me, anyway. You could still buy a solid dinner for two shillings then.

"Oh, I should have held onto it in India," she said. "But I thought the English were so honest."

By this time the Cockney cleaning woman had heard us

talking and came up. "Lost your purse, love?" she asked. "I saw that purse, and I almost called out to you. Is it gone?"

Hansa repeated her lament to the cleaning woman. "I thought students in England could be trusted," she said.

"For that matter, love, it may not 'ave been a student. We're open to the street. Almost anybody could come in, and it's so early in the term we shouldn't know they didn't belong here."

What the woman said was true. The College faced on the Strand, and anybody might well walk in, although I myself had walked up and down the street several times before I located the College. Repairs were still going on for wartime bomb damage, and the presence of construction seemed to hide it. But a Londoner would know where it was.

"It may turn up, of course," the woman said. "You can ask me again, and the man at the front door. Look after her, ducks," she said to me. "See she doesn't leave things around again."

"I'll try," I said, smiling at the notion that I might be expected to look after anyone here in London. It was all I could do to look after myself. Sackville, New Brunswick and Kingston, Ontario, where I had been a graduate student at Queen's, were the limits of my experience, and London was certainly a change from either of them.

"Do you need a little cash?" I asked. "I haven't much with me, but I could lend you a pound."

"Five shillings is enough. I have some in my room, but I need a little for lunch. Do you know, I don't even remember your name, though you did tell me."

"Lorna," I told her, "Lorna Ridley."

"As in *Lorna Doone*?"

It was typical, I realized later, that she tried to connect my name with a book.

Deciding against the College cafeteria, we had lunch together at a small, cheap lunch counter in the Strand. Sandwiches, cake, bitter coffee. Not a very good lunch. Although she was still disturbed by the loss of her handbag, Hansa recovered somewhat. "Imagine having lunch on the Strand," she said. "Doesn't it make you think of Samuel Johnson? He used to walk here. And we're a stone's throw from Fleet Street. And St. Clement Danes and oranges and lemons."

Her brown eyes sparkled, and a smile lingered around her mouth. She was younger, I decided, than I had thought.

I felt that way about the Strand, too, but in a way I was surprised that she did. What about Indian independence? Didn't she think of the British as wicked oppressors? My father's family had come, a long time ago, from Suffolk, and I intended to go sometime to see where they came from. "Blood's thicker than water," my father always said; and I thought it was blood that was calling me. But Hansa was not returning to the land of her ancestors.

She was however, it seemed, coming to a land of spiritual ancestors. She had been brought up, almost more than I had, on English books, and her mental map of England was a literary map, remarkably well filled in. Strange that she expected all English people to be honest. She might have expected London to be full of Dickensian pickpockets instead. "Of course I shouldn't have been quite so trusting," she admitted, "but they do seem honest. Look at the way they leave the newspapers out and people leave the right change and take one. They couldn't do that in India. The money and the papers would both disappear."

We exchanged information on each other. She was married but had no children. She taught English at a women's college in Bombay; her husband worked for the wireless and was a poet. Yes, of course she would miss him, but she had wanted for years to come to England for graduate work. It was the dream of a lifetime. Yes, it was for me too, I said.

I was here on a scholarship from home. Sometimes I was wildly excited; sometimes, I admitted, I was homesick. I didn't mention Benny, my boyfriend back at Queen's. After all, we were not yet officially engaged.

Hansa's handbag did turn up later that day, minus the money, but with all those keys and snapshots that people treasure. When we returned to the hostel at the end of the afternoon, she took me up to her room, which was packed with English books and oriental ornaments, and made tea for me. She had bought a little electric fire, on which she heated the water for the tea, and which made the room seem warmer and cosier. I made a mental note to myself to buy one when I got the next instalment of my scholarship; for, although the building was supposed to have central heating, not much heat ever came through.

"You've made your place more homelike than mine is," I said enviously.

Here, in her own territory, she did not seem the rather drab woman I had first thought her. When she took off her coat, in which she had stayed huddled all through class and lunch, she was wearing a rich sari, blue edged with silver, over a crimson top. The gold bangles on her wrists tinkled as she busied herself with the tea-things, and I noticed the rings on her long, graceful hands.

She seemed to grow taller, to walk with more dignity. She was the gracious, smiling, self-possessed hostess, serving me scented tea and biscuits that tasted of some unrecognizable flower, and offering me a cigarette (which I did not take) from an elaborately carved wooden box. I had not seen anybody like this back home in Sackville. Would the cleaning woman at King's suggest that I should look after Hansa if she saw her now? I thought not.

Shortly after that occasion I came down with a cold. I hadn't yet bought the electric fire for my room, and I couldn't seem to get warm, although I wore flannelette pyjamas and a heavy wool dressing gown. The house nurse visited me in my room, told me I was to stay in bed, and arranged that the girls on my corridor should take turns bringing me my meals. I hadn't talked to most of them before, and perhaps might have been slower becoming acquainted if I had stayed well. The friendliest were my two nearest neighbours, Daphne Lloyd and Martha Godwit, both undergraduates at University College. They arrived together, Daphne carrying a tray with the main course, Martha following with the sweet. Daphne, it was clear, was the lively one as well as the pretty one. She set down her tray with a flourish, flung the napkin over one arm, and pretended to be a professional waiter. Martha, who was as plain as her name, stood by smiling quietly at her friend's capers.

As they had already eaten dinner, they sat down and watched me eat, Daphne in the only armchair in the room, Martha in the hard chair at my desk. It was the evening for rabbit, which I would have found difficult to get down even if I had been well. I pushed it unhappily around the plate, managing to swallow some of the potatoes and brussels sprouts.

"Come on now, Lorna, you can do better than that," Daphne said. "How do you expect to live if that's all you eat?"

"Don't tease her, Daphne. She's just feeling ill. Maybe she can eat the sweet."

The sweet was a rather tough tart covered with lumpy custard sauce. I was struggling with it when there was a tap at the door and Hansa appeared. As Daphne and Martha had not met her before, her arrival distracted them from nagging me into eating, and I thankfully pushed the food aside.

Hansa managed to transform the occasion from a sick-room call to a party. She brought along her heater, and Martha toasted bread in a little wire toaster. We ate the toast with our ration of butter and some currant jam that Daphne's mother had sent her. I had a jar of instant coffee, and we heated water for coffee after we had demolished the toast. It was rather like breakfast, but better than that awful dinner.

Hansa and Daphne tended to dominate the room, Hansa by sheer physical presence, Daphne by a species of school-girlish high spirits. "I'm not English either," she told us. "My family is Welsh, look you." And her voice took on a singsong inflection, like an actor impersonating a Welsh-man.

"Don't be silly, Daffy," Martha said. "You know you only go to Wales in summer vac. Everybody comes from somewhere else."

Daphne by this time was sitting on the floor, having presented the armchair to Hansa. "Everybody but Martha comes from somewhere else," she said, dropping the stage Welsh accent. "Smashing toast, Martha. Good to have it hot for a change. I wish we had it hot for breakfast."

"It wouldn't be good for your character every morning, would it?"

"That's true. Cold toast, cold kippers, cold baths, cold rooms. They make the English character strong. That's why you rule all us lesser breeds like Welsh and Indians and Canadians, Martha."

"Rule you—I like that. Who made the toast for you just now, I should like to know? And the coffee?"

"Ah, that's ruling by service, you know. The iron hand in the velvet pot-holder."

"Well, Ducks, if I rule, I think we should all leave Lorna soon so she can get some sleep for her cold."

"Ah—after all, Martha calls me *dux*. I must be the leader. Why doesn't everybody laugh?"

"Because they haven't been corrupted by doing the *Times* crossword every night as you do, Daphne."

To my annoyance, Hansa saw the joke before I did. And it seemed that she also was fond of doing the *Times* crossword. Which of us was more foreign? She did not say "elevator" for "lift" or "sidewalk" for "pavement" or "sick" for "ill." She never said "I will" when she meant "I shall." She never said "I guess." (But Chaucer used it, I told them.) People did not know at once when she opened her mouth that her rs and ows came from across the ocean. On the other hand, I did not say "Atchah!" when I was startled. And if I left my mouth shut I looked English.

Martha came back a few minutes after the others had left carrying a hot water bottle wrapped around with a towel. "We mustn't improve your character to the point where we kill you," she said. "I hope you're not too homesick. England can be chilly, but people don't usually die of the cold."

"Don't you need it yourself? Is your room warm?"

"Oh, this is an extra one. Don't worry."

If she was managing, I was glad at the moment to be managed. I woke up the next morning feeling much better, although the house nurse, who was also managing, insisted that I should stay in bed an extra day.

We got into the habit, after that, of eating breakfast and dinner together in the dining hall, Hansa and Daphne and Martha and I, and another young woman from India who lived on Hansa's floor. Savitri was a few years younger than Hansa. She was also married, and was getting a degree because her husband's mother wanted an educated daughter-in-law. She was a plump butterball of a girl, without Hansa's grace and dignity, always a shade breathless and a shade untidy.

I soon realized that, although Hansa and Savitri were polite and apparently friendly to each other, they had their differences. Each discussed the other with me over a cup of tea. "Hansa is a Parsee, not a Hindu," Savitri told me. "We think the Parsees are too Westernized and pro-English. It's not that we look down on Parsees exactly. They always have money and influence, they aren't like lower-caste people. But they're outsiders. It's unusual that she's married to a Hindu."

"She seems very intelligent," I said cautiously.

"Parsees are always clever," Savitri answered, as if she were making an accusation. Then she brightened, as she hit on what seemed to her a way of making things clear to me. "We feel about them the way you English people feel about Jews. They are always clever and have money too, but they are outsiders, aren't they?"

"I'm not English," I reminded her neutrally. "I'm Canadian. How do you know how English people feel about Jews? From Martha and Daphne?"

"Oh, no, not them. I've heard other people talking."

I might have said that Benny was Jewish; but Benny hadn't written very satisfactory letters lately. I didn't want to talk about him, in case he had disappeared into thin air. So I said, "Hansa's a very handsome woman. She dresses well."

"I think she overdresses. She has too many saris."

Hansa in turn was critical of Savitri. "She prattles too much," she said. "She's a gossip, and she's sloppy and lazy. But it's probably not her fault. It's her upbringing. Hindus can be maddening."

"But your husband is a Hindu, isn't he?"

"Yes. We have our troubles sometimes." It seemed for a moment as if she might say more, but she didn't.

Even though Hansa and Savitri disapproved mildly of

one another, the three of us went out together fairly often, sometimes for a meal in an Indian restaurant, sometimes to a play or a movie. We realized that we had more money to spend on such events than Daphne or Martha had. Sometimes Martha would come on a sightseeing trip with us, to an art gallery or to one of those literary shrines that so fascinated Hansa. (Savitri did not care for these trips to Dickens' house or Johnson's house or Carlyle's house.) All five of us got together for coffee parties in each other's rooms, especially when Hansa or Savitri or I had a food parcel from home.

"Austerity" was the catchword of the time. Postwar England was hungry and cold, and we seemed to spend much of our time thinking of how to make ourselves comfortable. We grumbled about our one boiled egg a week and the cold scrambled egg made from egg powder which we had one other morning. We grumbled about meatless sausages and about the inevitable mashed potatoes and limp brussels sprouts. I grumbled because I had no milk to drink. Hansa and I grumbled about heatless days in the British Museum, where we both frequently spent our afternoons, Hansa in the manuscripts section, I in the main reading room of the library. We all grumbled about the chill in our rooms, and Hansa and I grumbled about the fog, which smelled like smoke, and was sometimes a visible density floating in the corridors.

But we all adjusted in our various ways. I bought a thick red blanket to supplement the hostel blankets, and kept a bottle of sherry in my clothes cupboard, doling it out in cautious thimblefuls. Savitri discovered that she could sometimes buy a fowl without ration points, and cooked us up a curry in the little kitchenette at the end of the corridor. Hansa wore extra layers of clothing over and under her sari. Once, when I came to her door at bedtime to borrow an aspirin, I saw the pile of clothing she had worn that day on her bed. "Good heavens, Hansa," I said, "do you wear all that? You should be a striptease artist. Think of the suspense of taking it all off. They could call your act the Dance of the Seventy Veils or the Extra-Mysterious East."

Christmas was coming. Savitri planned a trip to Glasgow to visit some relatives of her husband. Martha invited Hansa and me for Christmas. Hansa accepted the invitation, but I refused. I was determined to be homesick, and did not want to be distracted by friendly faces. I would go off by myself to a place I didn't know and indulge myself in homesick thoughts of my family and of Benny, who rarely answered my letters.

I chose Minehead, in Somerset, as a place that looked southerly on the map, and made reservations at a small hotel that Daphne recommended. After all, I was not really very homesick, once I was away from London and could take walks on the neighbouring moor. The meals, even in that very moderate hotel, were better than in the university hostel, and the sea air made me hungry. I had some bad moments on Christmas day itself. It was the first Christmas I had not spent with my family in Sackville, and I choked a little over my midday meal. But a long walk in the afternoon revived me, and when I came into the lounge late in the afternoon I was ready for tea by the fire.

Something was familiar about the young man sitting with his back toward me reading one of the hotel magazines. When he looked up I realized that I really did know him. "George Kennedy!" I exclaimed. "What are you doing here?"

I had known him slightly at Queen's and had forgotten that he also had come to Britain, but to Edinburgh instead of London. I suppose he had even more reason than I to pick a southerly town for part of his Christmas vacation.

He was no great favourite of mine, but I looked at any Canadian in England with a certain warmth. We had our tea together.

"Have you and Benny broken up?" he asked me at some point in our conversation. "Seems to me someone told me they saw him out with Esther Levine."

"Esther Levine! She lives on chocolate sundaes and has two chins and only half a brain."

"Some like them fat. Anyhow he might just have bumped into her accidentally. A friend of the family, maybe."

"Well, there's no reason he shouldn't go out with her. We aren't engaged."

"Oh, I thought maybe you were. Practically."

"No, we're not," I said, with unnecessary sharpness.

So that's why he hasn't written, I thought bitterly. And I've been so faithful, spending all my time with a bunch of women. A lot of good it's done me.

There was a Christmas party at the hotel in the evening. The next day George and I walked to Dunster, the neighbouring village, admired the local castle and the yarn market, and stopped for tea and scones at a farmhouse on the way back. We laughed a lot over the tea, and the farm woman clearly thought we were young lovers. George, I decided, was better company than I had given him credit for back at Queen's. In the evening we went to a pantomime of Robin Hood. Neither of us understood all the jokes, but we were easily amused. In the last act George put his arm around me. I didn't find him as attractive as Benny, but if Benny was going out with Esther Levine why should I pine?

II

I arrived back in London on the afternoon of New Year's Eve. Most of the students were still away on vacation, but

Hansa was in town. She had enjoyed her visit to Martha's, she said, but had work she wanted to do.

We decided to see the New Year in together in my room. I lit candles and poured out ceremonial glasses of sherry. As the bells rang in the New Year, we touched glasses and wished each other well.

"A new decade," I said, "the fifties. Doesn't it sound strange? Where will we both be in 1960?"

I was thinking of myself, of Benny and George, of Sackville, New Brunswick, and maybe Toronto or Montreal.

"There is someone in Canada you want to go back to," Hansa said.

"There was," I answered, sighing. "I don't know if he's still there." I resolved to write very plainly to Benny and ask for the truth about Esther Levine.

"You're lucky," I said. "You're sure of your husband."

Suddenly I realized that Hansa was crying, her face absurdly scrunched up.

"Hansa," I exclaimed, "whatever is the matter?" And I got up and put my arms around her. "What is it? Tell me about it."

After a period when she wouldn't say anything, but sobbed inconsolably, she wiped her eyes and said, "It's my husband. He has another girl, and he wants to marry her."

In between bouts of sobbing, she told me about her marriage. There had been troubles from the beginning. All those quarrels about food, for instance. And in spite of the fact that this had been a marriage for love, a Western marriage in fact, not one arranged by their families (who of course had disapproved). Yet when she had left for this year in England she had thought everything was all right. He had seen her off for the voyage with such affection, had bought her lavish presents; her stateroom had been full of flowers. Now there was this girl, younger than Hansa of course, but not especially beautiful or charming. "Why, she's fat," Hansa said, unconsciously echoing my comment on Esther Levine. "And she's a Communist," she added. "How can he possibly marry a Communist?"

I burst out laughing. I suppose I must have seemed unsympathetic, but I couldn't help it. I had little interest in politics, and couldn't imagine anyone caring about his wife's politics.

"Perhaps it isn't as serious as you think," I said, sobering down. "Perhaps he'll be tired of the girl soon. Isn't he fond of you still?"

"Oh," she said in disgust, "he says he loves us both. He even suggested that I should stay on as his wife, that he could be married to both of us. Even the Hindus have given that up, most of them."

"I don't see why that would be so very dreadful," I said, trying to imagine what it would be like to be Esther Levine's co-wife. "At least you have a choice."

"No, I don't. It's absurd and humiliating. I don't see how a Westerner like you could possibly approve of it. Savitri wouldn't, I'm sure."

"Well, of course you know what you can put up with, Hansa. I may be a Westerner, but I don't think all Western institutions are perfect, including Western marriage."

What I had to say to Hansa was probably not much consolation, but perhaps talking about it helped her. Before she left the room she said to me, "Please don't tell the others. Especially Savitri. It would just be another piece of gossip for her. Eventually they will have to know, but not yet."

I promised her, told her to have a good sleep, and began composing my own letter to Benny in my mind.

The second term seemed to me shorter than the first, perhaps because the weather began to seem warmer as early as February. Theoretically I should have been miserable.

My letter to Benny, inquiring about Esther Levine, had finally received a response. He and Esther were indeed seeing quite a bit of each other. They might very probably marry. He didn't bother telling me, as Hansa's husband had told her, that he still loved me too. I spent a morning weeping about it when the letter came in the post, but dried my tears and took the tube over to South Kensington, where I wandered aimlessly around the Victoria and Albert Museum looking at collections of fans and snuffboxes. There were too many things in the world to see (even just fans and snuffboxes) for me to waste time being broken-hearted. Especially with spring coming. I made a resolution to be cheerful.

The beautiful, gradual English spring made it easier than it might have been for me to keep my resolution. London under that dappled blue sky renewed itself and put on fresh charms. I strolled about the bookstalls, bought daffodils at street corners, and noticed that grass was growing in the bombed-out area around St. Paul's. I realized with surprise that I had fallen in love with the city I had grumbled about all winter, even our grubby little Marchmont Street, with its sooty shops and its one dingy restaurant where working men ate beans or fish and chips for their five o'clock tea. I was no longer cold, I had become accustomed to brussels sprouts, and I knew how to calculate in English money. I was at home, even happy.

Hansa, however, was not so easily distracted from her misery. She was visibly losing weight; and, although she maintained a cheerful face before the others, she poured out on me her tears and her anger against her husband. I was sometimes dismayed by these outpourings, and worried that she would make herself genuinely ill. But I did what I could to distract her. I insisted that we go to the new plays. Savitri, Hansa and I trundled out to Whipsnade on a Sunday afternoon which unfortunately turned out rainy. I even tried to do the *Times* crossword with her.

I had more practical things to consider, however, than broken hearts, either Hansa's or my own. I had hoped to have my scholarship renewed for the next year, but failed to manage it. I had to find a job. I wrote a few letters to Canadian and American universities, but they seemed a long way off. Perhaps it would be easier to find something when I reached home. I would have liked to stay in England, but could not imagine finding a job here in London.

I discussed my problems with Hansa. After all, she discussed hers with me. She was sympathetic. "Would you be interested in teaching in India?" she asked one evening.

"I'd be interested in a job anywhere at this moment," I said. Then I added, "Yes, I'd especially like a job in India. It would be an adventure, a new place." My notions of India were derived just about entirely from Hansa and Savitri, or from reading *A Passage to India* and translations of the *Bhagavad-Gita* and the *Zend-Avesta*; but I felt that if I could live with Hansa and Savitri I could live with India.

A couple of weeks later she said to me, "There is a vacancy in my college in Bombay if you are really interested, and I am sure you could have it if I recommend you. Would you like to apply?"

This was something more definite and immediate than I had expected. "Well, yes, good, I'll apply, if you tell me what to say. I've had a couple of other nibbles, too, one in Alberta, one in Vermont. I should turn up something from one of them."

To my surprise, she seemed somewhat disturbed. "Yes, but if you apply at Bombay you must promise me to accept. If I recommend you, and then you accept another position, they will think you are unreliable and so am I."

"Really, Hansa, how could they think that? Some people

apply for dozens of jobs and then take the best offer. Everyone does it. And I suppose they will take the application they like best."

"That may be how North Americans think" (was there a faint edge of scorn in Hansa's voice?) "but I assure you it is not true in India. If you think you had rather teach in Vermont or Alberta, I shall not recommend you for Bombay."

"I don't prefer Vermont or Alberta, but I want to be safe and I don't want to be at a disadvantage. Suppose something really good turns up just after I've applied? How can I tell the other place I'm refusing it because I've applied to Bombay when I haven't even had an offer?"

"I don't see why not. Don't you trust me? If I recommend you, you are sure to have the offer. Do you think I don't tell the truth?"

"Of course you tell the truth, Hansa. There's no need to be emotional about it. But people who tell the truth are sometimes mistaken."

We went on arguing, or bickering, at great length. I did not see why I should be bound to accept a job because I applied for it; she did not see why I should not believe that, in this instance, an application was as good as an acceptance.

Finally I suggested that I have a little time to think it over and to write to my family. Rather grudgingly, Hansa agreed. It occurred to me that if all that fuss could be made about the application, I might find the job itself something of a headache.

When my mother wrote, it was in great agitation. She and my father could put up with my going off to Ontario and England, though they hadn't much liked that, but India was a different matter. A real foreign country. Surely I should be able to get something nearer home than that. If I went there, they might never see me alive again. After all, they were getting on. And so on.

If I had been sure enough of my own mind, I would not have worried about convincing my parents. But I was not sure. I wished that I had had some word from Vermont or Alberta. I decided that I had better tell Hansa that I would not apply for the job in Bombay. Hansa said little, but there was a perceptible chill in her manner. It is, after all, sometimes easier to forgive an injury than what one thinks of as the refusal of a favour.

The long Easter vacation was approaching. George Kennedy wrote me suggesting that I come to Edinburgh, but I refused—sensibly, I thought. Instead, I went to Suffolk for the first week of the vacation, to Aldeburgh, where my father's family had come from. Aldeburgh was colder than London at this time of year, with a constant chill wind blowing off the sea. Everybody told me I should have come in June, for the Festival. Nobody ever visited at this time of year. The hotel where I stayed was deserted except for a few elderly permanent residents, including an ancient army officer who had served in India, a retired sea captain, and one or two old ladies. I was polite to the old people, petted the hotel cat, went for long walks, and read a Trollope novel by the fireplace in the lounge in the evening. My room was too cold for habitation except when I was in bed with a hot water bottle.

But I enjoyed the dullness of the holiday. Especially I enjoyed walking in the flat, fenny landscape, which reminded me of the Tantramar marshes at home. I had the same consciousness of sky and space, of clouds shifting, converging and dispersing, over the drab fields. I walked and tried to imagine my future, but could not. I felt as if I would be happy to stay here forever, away from the necessity of making choices.

In one of the little curio shops, with its odds and ends of seashells and amber, I bought an amber necklace to take back to London for Hansa. I also bought a couple of postcards of the town, and wrote polite notes on them, one to George Kennedy at Edinburgh, one to Benny at Queen's.

Hansa and I had planned to spend the second week of the holiday together, visiting the Isle of Wight. We stayed in Shanklin, but took bus trips around the Island. Here, also, we were ahead of the season for visitors. I had been wary of this trip with Hansa, afraid she might be in a bad mood. However, she said to me cheerfully, "Those eighteenth-century people who went off on the Grand Tour to get over a disappointment were probably right. Travelling is a distraction."

I did not like the landscape as well as the Suffolk coast—I thought it was what I disparagingly called "picturesque"—but I was glad to find Hansa so ready to be pleased, so happy that Tennyson had lived on the island and Keats had visited it. When she took a snapshot of Carisbrooke Castle, I took a snapshot of her taking the snapshot.

Out for a walk from one village to another, we were surprised at lunchtime to encounter a little restaurant advertising Indian curries.

"Bless us!" Hansa exclaimed (and would anybody now say that except Hansa, I wondered?) "Who would expect anything like curries here?"

Inside, it was a dingy little place; but we found a corner table and studied the menu.

"Curried beef!" Hansa said, amused. "You would never get curried beef in India. Beef at all, for that matter."

That was the only curry on the menu, however, so we ordered it. After all, to Hansa the cow was not a sacred animal.

She pronounced it not bad, though decidedly English.

"How homesick it makes me, though," she said. "Perhaps you are right to want to go back to your own country."

She was, I supposed, forgiving me for not applying for the job in Bombay.

It was summer when I left England. I was sailing for Montreal tourist class on the *Empress of Scotland.* Hansa and Savitri, Martha and Daphne had all given me advice and help in packing. We had gone on a last celebrative trip to Hampton Court, where we had got lost in the maze and eaten strawberries at a table under a striped awning. We had done the *Times* crossword together on the last evening, in the midst of my packed suitcases, and promised solemnly to see each other in ten years' time.

I was up early in the morning for breakfast. The last morning for those meatless sausages. Martha ran out to the corner to call a cruising taxi, and the girls helped me with my suitcases. Savitri ran downstairs with my alarm clock, which I had forgotten, and put it into my hands at the last moment. Hansa came to the station with me.

Not much time. Into the station. The train. This compartment. I am settled. Hansa is outside, waving goodbye, and the train pulls off. For Liverpool.

I am now almost crying, and wish I had agreed to go to Bombay. I am slipping through English countryside for the last time. I must take a travel-sickness pill before the boat.

We are here. Do I have my passport, my vaccination certificate, my ticket, my money? Windy weather. I hope not a rough voyage.

There is George Kennedy, as I expected. Going home on the same ship.

No, I did not see Hansa again in ten years' time. I had only one letter from her, from London. I do not know what happened to her, though I once met someone who knew her husband's second wife. She may be dead. She may be remarried. Sometime, I think, I shall go to Bombay and inquire.

VOYAGE HOME

My clearest recollection of that voyage home on the *Empress of Scotland* is of being seasick. It was the summer of 1950. I had just spent a year as a student in London, was returning home to Canada to an unknown future. I had only once before been on a ship, the previous autumn when I sailed from Montreal to England. On that earlier trip, we entered gently on our voyage. I had not even noticed the moment at which we had moved away from the dock; and our leisurely trip down the St. Lawrence to Quebec had accustomed me to the motion of the ship before we reached the Atlantic. I had mailed my parents in Sackville, New Brunswick and my boyfriend Benny in Kingston, Ontario last-minute shipboard notes from Quebec, rather boastfully proclaiming that I had not yet been a bit seasick; and, although I had had a day of feeling queasy later, I had maintained a moderately good appetite most of the way across.

Things were different coming back, however. The *Empress* hit rough seas almost as soon as she was out of sight of land. I awoke in the middle of the night, that first night out, with the ship pitching and rolling desperately, as it seemed to me. I was in an upper bunk in my tourist cabin, and wondered if I might fall out. On my previous trip, I had been lucky enough to secure a lower bunk; but this time, as the youngest of the four women in the cabin, I was obviously doomed to an upper.

The two women in the lower bunks were the Miss Crawfords, elderly spinster sisters from Scotland, on their way to visit relatives in Toronto. The other woman, in the bunk opposite me, was a hearty, bouncy Englishwoman somewhere in her late thirties, Muriel Carter by name. I had taken an instant dislike to Muriel, perhaps because she had taken an instant liking to me, and had said to me, "Of course we must put our names down for the same table, Lorna. That's the sensible thing." I had really expected to eat my meals with George Kennedy, a Canadian I had known at Queen's, who was also going home on the *Empress*. I had not known how to refuse Muriel, and George had clearly been rather intimidated by her. We had eaten together that first night, but neither George nor I was talkative that evening; the bad weather might have contributed to our constraint. There were two other people at our table, a Canadian civil servant who had been visiting relatives in England and his twenty-year-old daughter. They also seemed subdued. Muriel was chatty enough for all of us, and kept up a constant flow of prattle about the ship, the food, the weather, the other passengers and the brother in Alberta whom she planned to visit. The roast beef made her think of her brother's ranch, which she had not yet seen.

Now, awakening in my upper bunk, I was aware of the heavy weight of that roast beef on my stomach, and of my stomach pitching and rolling with the ship. The two ladies from Scotland also seemed to be awake and suffering. Muriel, the only one of us in good health, rang for the stewardess, who looked in on us with a harried air and handed out seasickness pills and ginger ale.

The next morning the two Scottish ladies and I stayed in bed while Muriel went off to the dining-room for breakfast. I contented myself with tea and dry toast, and lay in my bunk as quietly as I could, watching the ceiling pitching with the motion of the ship. Muriel, when she came down again, reported that the storm was supposed to be a "moderate gale" and that not many people were around. Could she do anything for the rest of us? If not, she was off to write letters in the lounge.

I could not help, in between bouts of seasickness, contrasting the present stormy sea with the more peaceable voyage last fall. But then everything had been different. At that time I had been travelling to a country I had never seen, looking forward to what I hoped would be an adventure. I had expected to miss Benny, and of course Canada, but I had thought they would both be there, safe and unchanged, when I came home. Now I was on my way to Sackville, New Brunswick. My adventure was over; I did not have a job to return to; and Benny was going with another girl. Even without a gale blowing, I might have felt seasick.

The one hopeful feature of the voyage was that George was on board. I had known George slightly in Kingston, where he and Benny and I had all been graduate students at Queen's. George had studied in Edinburgh during my year in London. We had met by chance on a Christmas vacation in Somerset; we had exchanged some letters; and, although I had refused to go to Edinburgh for Easter when he asked me, I had rather enjoyed his company when he came to London himself in late spring. I still thought of myself as in love with Benny; but I considered myself to be a practical girl, and did not imagine myself as being eternally faithful to Benny if he married someone else. Although George was going back to Edinburgh in the fall, he was coming home to Canada for the summer. We planned to travel home on the same ship; and I expected to see George daily on the trip. Unless, of course, we were both seasick all the way. Muriel reported to me that he was not up for breakfast or lunch but put in a brief appearance for dinner.

The next day the storm had subsided somewhat. The ship merely rolled, instead of both pitching and rolling. The two Scottish ladies rose from their bunks and prepared shakily to go on deck for breakfast. I was still mildly queasy, however, and felt that I would rather lie quietly and eat lightly than go to all the exertion of finding my way to the dining-room.

The Miss Crawfords, once they had managed to leave the cabin, decided to stay up on deck; but Muriel, who I think felt guilty leaving me by myself, kept popping down unexpectedly to inquire if I needed anything. Would I like a detective story? A crossword puzzle book? Some chewing gum? Shouldn't I try to come up on deck, just for half an hour? The salt air would do me good.

She made herself comfortable on the opposite bunk, and began to question me about Canada. Was my home near Alberta? No? Had I visited it, then? What was it like? Bert, her brother, thought it was the greatest place on earth. He had come out to Canada right after the War; had lived in

Toronto for a while, but had not cared for it; but he had moved west to Alberta, had prospered there, and married a Canadian girl. He had sent Muriel the money for the passage out, and she had quit her office job in Manchester, packed her possessions, and intended, if she liked the country, to stay, as she said, "for good."

"Bert tells me I'll have more chance of getting a man in Alberta than I'd have at home," she said. "Do you think that's true?"

I thought her too ancient to be interested in men, and imagined that at her age I should be content to settle back and knit and watch younger people holding hands.

"Hunting for men isn't something I'm good at," I told her.

"What about your boyfriend at the dinner table, young Mr. Kennedy?" she asked.

"He isn't my boyfriend, he's just a friend."

"Oh, we all know what that means," she said, laughing. "I'll wager you and he are the best of friends."

I didn't bother answering; and Muriel, after a few more attempts at conversation, went out on deck and left me to sleep.

In the afternoon she appeared again, with a masculine figure behind her. "Look who's here to cheer you up," she said gaily, and I realized that she had George in tow. I was not altogether grateful for the attention. I did not look my best, and might have preferred to wait until evening, when a dab of make-up and the presence of artificial light would have made me appear healthier. However, I tried to smile and be pleasant. After all, it was thoughtful of George to come and inquire after me. Or had Muriel compelled him to come? I was conscious of the fact that I was wearing silly pyjamas figured with pink and blue sailboats, and I drew the covers close around my chin to hide them from view.

That evening I did struggle up for dinner, although I ate little and could not attend to the conversation. My stomach had settled down, but my head was throbbing in unison with the ship's engines. George and Muriel both seemed cheerful, however, and George said to me after dinner that he thought Muriel was quite a card. The civil servant and his daughter were still in their cabins, and didn't appear until the next day.

By our third day out the weather was clear, the ocean gentle, and all the passengers up on deck for our Sunday morning boat drill. I was persuaded to attend a church service in the lounge with Muriel and the Miss Crawfords. George was not there, but our civil servant, Mr. Hardy, was. The two Crawfies, as Muriel called them, were disturbed when one of the hymns sung was "For Those in Peril on the Sea." I rather agreed with them, and thought the chaplain tactless in choosing it; but Muriel sang it with hearty enjoyment. Mr. Hardy recalled that it was sung during the War when he crossed in the same ship, then a troop ship. "That was a different voyage, all right," he told us over Sunday lunch. "We were all packed together like sardines, troops sleeping on the floor in the first class lounge. They kept us down below as much as they could, and the portholes were covered up. We all thought about submarines, though we didn't talk of them. And it was January, rough all the way. I could feel the ship roll for a day after I got to dry land."

Muriel listened sympathetically. She and Mr. Hardy had both been in London during the blitz, and compared experiences of near-escapes and memories of walking around lost in the darkened city. "But it was good for us," Muriel said, "made us more friendly. People talked to each other who would never have talked before. I don't suppose it'll last, though. We're stodgy, we English."

"Don't say that, Miss Carter," Mr. Hardy said. "You

aren't stodgy."

"Call me Muriel," she said, laughing. "I may not be stodgy now, but I was once. You should have known me before the War."

Muriel and Mr. Hardy (his name was Bob, but I could never think of him except as Mr. Hardy) seemed to find more to talk about than the rest of us did. They went off for a walk together on deck after lunch, while George, Fanny Hardy and I looked uncertainly at each other.

"I'm glad Miss Carter is so good at drawing Dad out," Fanny said. "I've had the most awful time with him since Mother died."

Her mother, she told us, had died last year, of cancer. It had been a hard death to watch, and her father had needed this change, a visit to England to see relatives and some friends of his Army days, as a distraction. It had helped him, she thought, but she had not enjoyed the trip herself. She had worried about him too much. Muriel Carter had seemed to make him more interested in conversation than he had been for a long time.

George, I could see, was touched and sympathetic. My sympathy would have been greater if his had been less.

Time on board ship seems longer than it is. We seemed suspended in an ocean of time as wide as the unbroken expanse of water on which our eyes rested. Early voyagers sometimes took months to cross this ocean. Now it took less than a week; but it seemed an exceptionally protracted week. There was time for hours of sitting on deck, wrapped in a blanket against the mid-Atlantic chill. There was time for strolling, singly or in twos or threes, watching those peculiarly flamboyant oceanic sunsets or the rise of the moon over the water. There was time for what I thought of as the rather stupid distractions of shipboard games, which Muriel and Mr. Hardy enjoyed together. We all went to a movie one evening, and were amused that it was about life on shipboard. There was more than the usual time allotted for eating and drinking. The deck stewards seemed always to be bringing around mugs of soup or tea and sandwiches, in addition to those three heavy meals a day. I wonder we did not all double our weight on the trip.

We were rather awed, as we came nearer the New World side of the Atlantic, to catch a glimpse one morning of an iceberg sailing away in the distance. Muriel saw it first, when we were dressing for breakfast, and pointed it out to me through the porthole. It was distant and strange, like a dream, shining in the sunlight; and if a traveller from another world who did not know what it was had seen it, he would have wanted to turn the ship and sail in pursuit of something so graceful and diamond-pure.

"I didn't know an iceberg could be so beautiful," I said, in surprise.

"Well, icebergs may be beautiful," Muriel said, shivering, "but I can't imagine anybody wanting to cuddle up to one."

We all talked about the iceberg at breakfast. Mr. Hardy was old enough to remember the headlines when the *Titanic* sank, and how that big floating world was wrecked by an iceberg that probably looked as innocent as ours. That was our coldest day on board. I remember putting on my thickest sweater and my warmest coat to go walking on deck. Muriel and the Hardys and George stayed inside and played cards together. How could they, in such cold exultant air?

We were all out on deck, however, on the last day of the voyage. We had left the Atlantic behind us and were sailing up the St. Lawrence to Montreal. The voyage had become a river excursion, a holiday picnic trip past green fields and pleasant villages clustered around white country churches. I had not realized before that I had been homesick for Canada, and was happy that people who had never seen it before should see it for the first time in such a glow of summer sunlight.

Muriel and I took a last walk together before dinner on our final evening. She had made an extra effort with her dress, I saw, and had flung a pale blue stole over her shoulders. Her face seemed softened; and she had acquired a certain dignity, even beauty. I noticed for the first time that her blue eyes were rather pretty.

"Bob Hardy is a good man," she said to me abruptly, as if I had asked her to confide in me. "I don't know what will come of it, and maybe nothing will, but I'm glad I met him."

I did not know how to respond to such directness. Perhaps she sensed that I had thought her a scheming woman, out to catch a vulnerable widower like poor Mr. Hardy.

She paused reflectively, then continued, "My boyfriend was killed in the War. I don't suppose I feel about Bob just the way I did about Ken, but then I don't suppose I'm as beautiful as the way he remembers his wife, either. You have to go on living, don't you?"

"I hope it works out for you," I said awkwardly, groping for words, and ashamed of how I had felt about her. "I hope you have the life you want."

"Oh, I don't want an ideal life. Just somebody to look after. Everybody isn't like that, but I'd have to have somebody to take care of, even if it was just the two Crawfies."

The Hardys and George were waiting for us at the table when we went in to dinner. I could see Mr. Hardy's eyes light up when they rested on Muriel. I wondered how Fanny would take to her as a stepmother.

Who, I wondered, would have thought, looking at our group, at Muriel and Fanny and me, that Muriel Carter would be the one woman at our table to be involved in a shipboard romance?

FLOWER GIRL

I don't know why I thought of Elaine this morning. It is nearly twenty years since I last saw her, and she never played an important part in my life. Perhaps somebody on a bus or a street corner resembled her slightly. Perhaps a student magazine, filled with rather amorphous but occasionally promising poems and stories, reminded me of her. At any rate, I woke up from a dream in which Elaine floated before me, a slight figure with a youthful, rather ecstatic face, large brown liquid sensitive eyes, and long waving chestnut hair falling down her shoulders, a flower tucked behind her ear.

People who admired Elaine were likely to compare her to fawns, does, or other such innocent and delicate creatures. I found myself at times hastily pushing back comparison to a spaniel, but then I was not as susceptible as some others to Elaine's charm, though I admitted its existence.

I first encountered Elaine when she was sixteen and I was twenty-six. The year was 1950.

I had lately returned to Fredericton from England after several years away from Canada. My father had died, and I had come back to live with my mother in the house on Charlotte Street where we had lived before, but which seemed now oddly changed and empty. I had had trouble getting a job, but eventually took one as a typist in the office of a local law firm. I hated the work, which I thought beneath me, and was inefficient at it. I was suffering from the emotional after-effects of a not very happy love affair, and felt tired, bruised and listless. I was extremely unhappy, and exaggerated the importance of the defunct love affair in the total picture of my unhappiness. The fact that I could not imagine loving anyone again, and that I felt hopelessly unlovable, was possibly of some importance in my misery; but there were certainly other causes for it. After life in the great grey city with its crowds of strange faces, its huge shops (magnificent even in those days of austerity to a naïve young person from a Canadian small town), its theatres and art galleries and historic buildings, I found it hard to come back to the dull little town on the quiet river where the neighbours all knew me and the only place of amusement was the local movie house. I had enjoyed Fredericton as a student going to high school and university, but then I had had my set of friends to go around with. Most of these had now gone off to jobs or marriages in other towns. Those who remained had developed other friendships and different interests. I felt left out and distinctly sorry for myself.

I still had two fairly close friends from my old university class in town, Ruth Somerville, another Fredericton girl, who taught in the local high school, and Eddie Sayers, who was now a very junior lecturer in English at the university. Ruth and Eddie were in process of becoming engaged, in their leisurely way, but now and then took me out for a drive or a dinner or a picnic. I had confided to Ruth some of the details of the unhappy love affair, and I suppose they felt sorry for me.

We had all three been members of a small informal group of students which had met to show each other our earnest efforts at poems and short stories and which had started a little mimeographed magazine. I was the only one of the three who still sometimes had stories published in little magazines, although Eddie now and then diverted himself with a rhyme.

It was through Ruth that I first met Elaine. Elaine was in Ruth's class in high school. Like many adolescents (though perhaps not as many then as now) she filled her scribblers with poems when she should have been doing algebra, and showed the results to Ruth. Ruth was sympathetic, and thought the poems rather more promising than the average.

When Elaine saw a story of mine in a magazine she took it to Ruth in great excitement. Did this author really live right here in this town, and did Ruth know her?

When she discovered that Ruth did know me, that in fact we were close friends, she was immoderately thrilled. She inflated my very minor achievement into a major one, and saw me as a famous author and a glamorous older woman who had lived in far places. She begged Ruth to introduce her to me.

Ruth was amused. "You have a great fan," she said to me, laughing. "Would you mind very much meeting her? You may find all that admiration cloying, but on the other hand it might be good for your ego. And perhaps you might be able to help her."

Elaine came to the door the next evening, with a note from Ruth, who had not been able to come with her. My mother was out at a church group, and I was reading a travel book and feeling bored.

The doorbell seemed to have a rather diffident ring, and the girl on the doorstep had a diffident air, although also an air of muted enthusiasm. She was rather incongruously clothed in a long, flowing, flowered dress combined with dirty saddle shoes, but there was no denying that she was beautiful. She carried a large scribbler under one arm which I apprehensively decided must be full of poems. I was right, of course. I made tea for her, and offered her some of my mother's date cookies. She seemed disconcerted because I was waiting on her, and seemed to think that I ought to be sitting in the most comfortable chair in the room while she stood respectfully at attention.

"You should let me wait on you, Miss Howard," she said. "After all, I'm younger."

This remark did not endear her to me. At thirty-six one may be amused when one's juniors treat one as infinitely older; at forty-six one may be resigned; but at twenty-six I was not used to such an attitude and did not enjoy it. I saw myself rapidly becoming an old maid; and I feared this prospect almost as much as I feared threats of atom bombs or famine. To be stuck for a lifetime in that horrible little office typing up wills, deeds and writs of execution was a possibility which seemed almost too much of a probability, and more than I could stand. Even the fat, fortyish, stupid second partner in the law firm seemed a preferable escape.

But Elaine had not meant to be catty. She was genuinely respectful of what she thought to be my superior experience, sophistication and distinction. She was overwhelmingly, absurdly admiring, and I thawed a little in the warm glow of her admiration.

She read me some of her poems aloud. On the whole, they were undistinguished, although now and then, whether by happy chance or genuine talent, there was a good line, a line which showed a true personality at work. The personality was perhaps too enthusiastic, too conventionally poetic, almost too sweet for my taste, but it was a real personality nevertheless. I told her which lines I liked, gave her some cautious encouragement and pointed out some obvious flaws. She left with profuse expressions of thanks and two or three books of poems tucked under her arm.

I did not expect to see much of her after that, but every few weeks she turned up with a fresh lot of poems and went away with another book to read. She successively imitated Emily Dickinson, Emily Brontë, W. H. Auden and Dylan Thomas, though I don't think she liked any of them quite so well as she liked Shelley and A. E. Housman. I was disconcerted at Christmas when she gave me a present, a scrolled, ugly gift book copy of the *Rubaiyat*, with an embarrassingly devoted inscription. I pretended delight, and hid the book in the back row of one of the bookcases after she had left the house.

"Really," I said to Eddie, who had come around with Ruth to look at our Christmas tree and drink a glass of sherry with my mother, "you must help me a bit with Elaine. I can't take her by myself. After all, I'm a prose writer really. You're the one who likes to write poetry, or used to. And you teach the stuff. Why don't you look at her work?"

So Eddie, Ruth, Elaine and I all had dinner together one evening in January at the new hotel on Front Street. Some men might have felt uncomfortable as the only man in the group, but Eddie was happy. He liked women in groups and was comfortable with them.

Eddie was the same age as I was and a year younger than Ruth. Neither of us had ever treated him with great respect. To Elaine, however, he was an older man and a professor, and she treated his opinions with something approaching veneration. He was not, of course, in Elaine's view, quite as real an author as I was, but he was a genuine critic. Poor Eddie was naturally rather flattered by her attention, and began to expand and make profound pronouncements on poetry and how to write it. I had never suspected him of being pompous, but it floated across my mind that by the time he became a full professor he might well be. However, that was Ruth's problem, not mine.

Ruth, I thought, looked mildly dismayed. She remarked to me afterward, "All that respect and attention from a beautiful young girl—I don't think it was too good for Eddie. I never looked as young as that even when I was younger."

I was amused, in spite of my general sense of depression with life. "Perhaps I'd better see that Elaine gets all the guidance she needs from me, after all," I said, "though she'll probably be in Eddie's freshman class in a year or two anyway."

"In a year or two it won't matter," Ruth said decisively.

Elaine readily forgot about Eddie. She was content—more than content—with my advice, though I became bored and restless giving it.

It was a long, dreary winter. I continued in a state of desolation on account of what I considered to be my broken heart, though I suspect I was suffering chiefly from a severe case of boredom. I could hardly drag myself out of bed in the mornings; suffered from an aching back and a headache at work; listened morosely to the chatter of the two other girls who shared the office with me; occasionally burst into tears in the washroom; and sobbed myself damply to sleep at night. I yearned wildly for London and longed for letters from there that never came. I attempted at times to write, and composed the first halves of dozens of short stories, almost all about attempted suicides, but could never manage to finish any of them. I felt I was at the bottom of a deep pit, and that it was impossible I should ever be able to drag myself up out of it.

Elaine's visits were at least a distraction. Though I could not manage to write, she wrote copiously, if not always well. I hoped she was spending as much time on such matter-of-fact things as chemistry or French as she was on poetry. Her father, I gathered, was ambitious for her, and wanted her to do well at school and go to university. Her mother was dead and her father was a short-order cook at one of those small anonymous places that sell hamburgers and fish and chips. Now such a place would also sell pizza, but that was before the pizza craze. I remember once stopping for a grilled cheese sandwich that Elaine's father served me. "My little girl is sure fond of you," he said. "It's good of you to act like a mother to my little girl."

I smiled politely, but I felt annoyed. I didn't even particularly like Elaine, I thought. I certainly didn't feel like her mother. After all, she was only ten years younger than I was. She weighed more than I did, too.

I was getting very thin, as a matter of fact. I had become so unhappy that I could hardly bear to swallow food, and pushed it around on my plate, as I had when I was a child and had a teacher whom I disliked. My mother, who had been dazed by her recent widowhood when I first came home and had not much noticed me, began to notice and to look at me anxiously. "What's wrong, Patty?" she asked. "Isn't there enough sugar in the pie? Lemon always used to be your favourite."

"Nothing's wrong, Mother," I answered. "The pie's

lovely." I tried to push it down, and choked on it miserably.

Spring was coming. Perhaps I would feel better then. I walked beside the river watching the ice slide out. There would be green grass. The pale yellow, furry early leaves would come out on the trees.

Elaine was enraptured by spring. She wrote dozens of lyrics, mostly in the manner of Shelley. She went out picking wildflowers, and appeared at my door with bunches of violets and trilliums. I was amused and mildly exasperated, and felt even more depressed. I would have liked florist's blossoms sent by an admiring male around my own age. I did not want wildflowers delivered by an adolescent girl. However, I smiled with painful hypocrisy and arranged the violets nicely in a pottery bowl.

Ruth and Eddie had finally become officially engaged, and planned to marry in the fall. Their happiness added to my sense of desolation, and the beauty of the advancing season made it more painful. I wanted to go away, but had not the energy to plan to leave, to find another job in another town. I took walks in the evening across the Devon bridge, looking down at the water and wondering if I had the courage to jump. But of course I did not.

All that summer Elaine brought me flowers. I don't know if she had any idea that I was depressed. I never told her so, and it's remarkable how little people are able to guess each other's feelings unless they are told. She did not cook dinner for me, as my mother did.

In September an old friend of my mother's wrote and suggested a job in Toronto. It was an office job not much better than the one I had, but it was a little better and at least it was in another place. The job seemed to me to drop from the sky, though I don't suppose it did.

I took a couple of weeks off between jobs, taking long walks and buying a few new clothes. Something, not precisely happiness but a faint glow of hope, crept over me, and I began to move more briskly and be able to swallow my mother's cooking.

Ruth and Eddie, just back for the new term and shortly to be married, came to the station with my mother to see me off.

"I thought Elaine would be here with flowers to say good-bye," Ruth said, smiling.

"I told her I'd be leaving but I didn't say on which train," I answered, smiling a little in return. "I couldn't bear wild-flowers on the train."

I felt weighed down as it was. My mother had brought a bag of pears and thrust it at the last minute into my hand. The pears were overripe and I was not quite sure what I could do with them. I certainly didn't intend to eat them, but perhaps some children might be sitting near me.

Eddie settled my hand luggage in the rack over my head. "Do you have something to read?" he asked. "Henry James, is it? Can you concentrate on all those subordinate clauses on a train?"

"All aboard," the conductor called. My mother and Ruth kissed me good-bye on the cheek. Eddie shook hands. They all got off, waving.

They stood together outside. Eddie's mouth was a little open. They waved again. Then they turned away. Ruth put her arm momentarily around my mother's shoulders. It flashed through my mind that my mother was becoming older than I had thought.

The train lurched forward. I opened my copy of *The Portrait of a Lady*. I did not intend to think too much of the people back there in Fredericton or the people in London either. I was beginning a new life.

Ruth wrote to me later: "Your friend Elaine was very much disappointed that she did not see you off. She told me that she had heard you were leaving, but thought it was on the next train. She thought you might have liked a flower for your buttonhole."

I felt a sense of relief, mixed with a mild guilt, that I had managed to avoid her.

Somehow or other, I did not get back to Fredericton for over two years. My mother had moved to Halifax, where she had relatives, and when I paid a family visit it was therefore to Nova Scotia rather than to New Brunswick. I was rather busy, moderately happy, and not too eager to seek out a town where I had last been distinctly miserable. However, in the autumn of 1953 I stopped off in Fredericton on my way back to Toronto from Nova Scotia.

I had dinner with Ruth and Eddie, who were settled in an apartment upstairs in an old house near the university. They had a baby and a dog, and were thoroughly domesticated.

We talked of old times and old friends, and worked our way through news of classmates and neighbours.

Eddie's younger brother, Norman, was in town then, in his third year at university, and wandered in for half an hour after dinner. He was a shy boy, better looking than Eddie, but without his ease with women. He talked chiefly to the dog and the baby, and seemed to ignore the rest of us, although he efficiently polished off a plate of food and a cup of coffee that Ruth brought in for him.

After he left, Ruth said to me, "You'll never guess who Norman's in love with, Patty."

"Is he in love?" I asked. "I don't suppose I know anyone Norman knows."

"Oh, come—an old friend of yours. You should be able to guess."

"Does he like his elders, then? All my old friends must

be eight or ten years older than he is."

"No—she's a year or so younger than he is. Surely you remember? Your old friend Elaine?"

"Elaine? Little Elaine Chase? The flower girl? She did get to university then, I take it?"

"Yes, she's just started her second year. A very bright girl, they say. Bright and beautiful too. It isn't fair, is it?"

"Well—and is she in love with Norman? He's a handsome boy, if perhaps a bit silent."

"Yes, she's in love with Norman," Eddie said. And then, a shade sourly, "She's also in love with at least six other boys, but especially in love with one thick-witted lunkhead whose family has too much money. Danny Etherege, if you've heard of the Ethereges."

"I haven't, but then I'm always failing to have heard of rich, important people."

"Well—rich, but not important. He's also Norman's best friend, through some failure of taste on Norman's part."

"That's inconvenient, isn't it? Being in love with his best friend's girl?"

"Oh, I don't suppose so. She probably goes to bed with all of them. The younger generation," he said gloomily, "is not as proper as we were."

I could not help laughing. I had suspected that Eddie might become pompous, but I hadn't expected the fate to overtake him for a few years yet.

"Don't sound so old just because you have a wife and baby, Eddie," I said. "After all, they're only eight or ten years behind us. They can't really be a new generation, can they?"

"There is a new generation every ten years," he said with finality. "I read that somewhere only the other day."

"Maybe you should make it seven or nine," I said. "At

least those are magic numbers. Ten isn't."

Two years later I was back again, in the summer. Eddie and Ruth had moved from the apartment to their own house, complete with mortgage, and invited me to stay with them. They now had two children, the second of whom had been named for his Uncle Norman. Norman, it seemed, had graduated that May and was going on to graduate work in history in Toronto. Perhaps I might see him now and then in the fall.

"Is he still in love with Elaine?" I asked.

"Elaine?" Ruth echoed. "Oh, Elaine's married and quit university, over a year ago now. I hear she had to—some truck driver or other. Everybody was terribly surprised."

"What about the wealthy young man—what was his name? Something like an Easter egg?"

"Danny Etherege. Well, of course the Ethereges would never let him marry her. I mean a cook's daughter, after all, and it wasn't as if she'd acquired the right sort of air, even. I mean, she was beautiful, but beauty isn't enough except in fairy tales. Danny's mother told him if he married her he wouldn't have any money, that was all. So he started going out with another girl, and Elaine went off and married the truck driver practically immediately."

"Why the truck driver? Why not Norman? Or was Norman not interested any more?"

"I don't know. Norman doesn't tell us much. I suppose it was a gesture. Well, she always was a queer girl."

I forgot about Elaine. Ruth and Eddie were almost the only people who wrote to me from Fredericton, and I suppose Elaine dropped out of their little world when she married her truck driver. Anyway, Ruth's letters were mainly concerned with the family news, Eddie's promotion, the new car, the children (now two girls and the boy), maybe a movie at the Gaiety or a book she had just read.

I visited them again in 1959. They had just bought a summer cottage on a lake outside town, and I was driven down to see it. Ruth and I sunned on our blankets, equipped with lotions and straw hats, while we kept an eye on the children, Theodora, young Norman, and Deirdre. (Eddie liked rather fancy names for girls. "Suppose they marry somebody named Smith or Jones?" he said. "They have to have something to distinguish them.") The older Norman had only lately visited them, Ruth said.

"That reminds me," she went on. "An old friend of yours died lately."

"A friend of mine that reminds you of Norman? Danny Easter-Egg, is it? I saw him lately, in Ottawa with his wife, and he looked quite well. But he's not a friend of mine."

"Feminine, I meant. Of course you remember Elaine, don't you?"

"Elaine? But whatever happened? She's—why, how old would she be? She'd just be twenty-five, wouldn't she? She was ten years younger than I am."

"I don't know what happened, really. She'd just had her fourth child. Maybe something went wrong after that. I'm not sure what it was."

"Fits," Eddie, who had just come up to us in his bathing suit, said. "The girl had a fit. She was an epileptic."

"Oh, Eddie, she did not have fits. I'm sure it wasn't a fit," Ruth said, laughing in spite of herself.

We talked, half sadly and half with a mild, morbid pleasure, about poor Elaine, who had died young. We were still, after all, moderately young ourselves. The beautiful hot sun burned down on us; the water rippled coolly. It was good to be alive, to be tanning luxuriously, to be able to get up and run into the cold shock of the lake. How sad to be like poor Elaine, finished forever with these delicious pleasures.

The dead are ageless. They haunt the nooks and corners of the minds of the survivors, a perpetual seventeen. They never grow old, but they do fade away. The smile dims, the chestnut hair grows pale, the figure becomes cloudier, more misty. It visits less often.

Six years later I was in Fredericton again. I had gone to a party, and found myself talking with a young man who looked faintly familiar, a rather handsome young man with brown eyes. I tried to think where I might have met him before. Probably, I decided, he was somebody's younger brother.

"Do you come from Fredericton?" I asked.

"I don't live here now," he said, "but I have relatives in Fredericton. That's why I especially wanted to meet you. My cousin was a great admirer of yours."

"Who was that? I haven't had too many great admirers. I cherish them."

"She was Mrs. Fred Gavin—Elaine Chase before she was married."

"Elaine," I exclaimed. "You're a cousin of Elaine's? That's why you looked familiar."

"Yes, people say I look like her. Elaine really thought you were wonderful, you know. She used to talk about you a lot. I guess she wanted to be like you. She wanted to write, to be different from other people. It was too bad life got her down."

"She died young, didn't she? I remember being startled when I heard."

"I was surprised myself, though I shouldn't have been. She used to talk to me a lot that last spring. She rather confided in me. I think sometimes I should have been able to do something, anyway say something to somebody who could have done something, but I was only fifteen then myself. I guess I just couldn't handle it."

"Why, what could you have done? I thought she died

after childbirth."

"No. The youngest was a month old. Didn't you hear, then? Elaine killed herself. She took an overdose of sleeping pills."

"I hadn't known, no. Why did she do that?"

"Oh, I suppose a number of reasons. Her marriage wasn't all that happy. Oh, don't get me wrong. Her husband wasn't a bad sort. His second marriage is happy, and the children are getting on fine. But Elaine was special, you know, a sensitive girl."

"That was the reason, then?" I asked. "An unhappy marriage, or unhappy for Elaine?"

"Well, I don't mean a miserable marriage, just not terribly happy. I don't suppose it was miserable, or they wouldn't have had four children, right one after the other. But that was another thing. She couldn't cope with all those children, so close together. She told me once that what frightened her was she was afraid she might get desperate some time and kill them. She said she'd kill herself rather than kill the children."

"That's what happened, then?" I felt dazed by all this information.

"Yes. I should have talked to someone, her husband or her father or my parents or someone. But I didn't believe her."

"They mightn't have believed either, might they? I don't see how you can blame yourself."

"Well, but she was such a beautiful person, Elaine was. She looked so beautiful. And she was nice to me. I used to write poetry then—kid stuff—and I would show it to her and she would criticize it. Intelligent criticism too. I really loved Elaine. You know how a kid can love an older woman?"

I looked at the young man with sudden surprise. Elaine as an older woman? To him I guess she was.

By this time I was working in Ottawa. Norman was also settled there, teaching at Carleton. He was a pleasant bachelor in his thirties who gave every indication of remaining a bachelor. We had struck up a friendship, not very demanding on either side, and he came to visit me now and then in my apartment on Metcalfe Street.

He visited me shortly after I got back from Fredericton. I made him coffee and a sandwich and noticed that he was beginning to gain weight. Elaine would have been worrying about a diet just about now, I thought, if she had lived.

"I met a cousin of an old friend of ours when I was in Fredericton," I said. "You remember Elaine Chase?"

He put down his cup with an expression of pain. "Of course I remember Elaine," he said. "How could I forget her?"

"Eddie and Ruth always said you were in love with her, but I never really knew."

"I was dreadfully in love," he said. "Dreadfully, hopelessly in love. And she never paid the slightest attention to me. It was Danny Etherege she wanted."

"That clod," I said. "I don't think he's anything like as attractive as you."

"Thank you, Patty, even though you don't mean it. He's got more on the ball than you give him credit for, though. He'll be in the Cabinet yet."

"Money, that's what he's got. And I suppose then he had muscle too, though he doesn't have it now. He didn't care for her, though, obviously."

"Oh, I wouldn't say that. They were both in love. It was so mutual it cheered you up to look at them, even though I was jealous."

"But he didn't love her as much as he loved money?"

"Or as he loved his family. Be fair, Pat. Anyway, he hadn't been brought up to make his own way. You and I never expected a lot from our parents. We could manage without it. But I don't know whether Danny could have managed. If he'd married Elaine and they had to live in two rooms while he worked at a pokey little job, and she had three or four kids one after another, she might just as likely have killed herself as she did with the man she did marry."

"You knew that had happened, then? I didn't know till the cousin told me. Eddie had said she had fits."

Norman smiled involuntarily. "That's our Eddie," he said affectionately. "Always full of information, even when not exactly true."

We went to a concert together a few nights later. "Ruth's worried about young Norman," I told him at intermission. "He's having trouble at school already. Ruth says she wishes he was more like his namesake."

"Sensible boy," Norman said. "He's just as well off not being like me."

He took a scrap of paper out of his wallet. "Look," he said. "After you were talking to me the other night I went home and rummaged around and found this. I thought you might be interested."

I took it from him curiously. It was an old newspaper clipping, crumpled and already somewhat yellowed, containing a brief notice of the sudden death of Mrs. Fred Gavin, the former Elaine Chase. It listed the mourners: her husband, her four children, her father, aunts and uncles. The funeral was to take place at Wilmot United Church. I read it nearly to the end, feeling that this young wife and mother was someone I had never met. And then I read the last line, and was suddenly struck, after all these years, by sorrow, pity, recognition, and something like amusement. I could not help reading the last line out loud: "No flowers, by request."

UNDERSTANDING EVA

Can I hope to understand Eva Fischer? Can the subject of psychoanalysis ever analyze the analyst? Why do I want to understand her, anyway? Isn't this attempt at understanding a proof that the old obsessive concern with her still exists? Or is it an indication that now, twenty years after the psychoanalysis, it has finally succeeded, and I am able to be detached from her? During that period of two years when I was visiting her, I certainly could not see her as herself. I saw her as mother, enchantress, witch doctor, quack, goddess. I depended on her. I loved her. I hated her. But only rarely did I glimpse her as a woman with hopes, fears, failings like my own.

At first I hardly saw her at all, except as someone who might help me. She was a psychoanalyst recommended by my doctor because I was suffering from headaches and tension. Why? I was a young unmarried woman without a lover, working at a boring job, and living with my parents in the rather dull Ottawa of the mid-1950s. (An incomplete explanation, but it will do well enough.) I had recently become a Catholic, and my parents disapproved of the conversion.

"Mrs. Fischer is a Catholic," my doctor told me when I mentioned this circumstance. "She is a Jungian psychoanalyst, has studied with Jung himself, I believe. You'll find her quite a personality."

I was late for my first appointment because I got lost on the way. Intentionally or unintentionally? Eva would probably have guessed intentionally, but I think not. I got off the Bank Street streetcar too soon and took a wrong turning.

The address was an apartment in a new highrise. The voice that answered my ring and told me to come up was thick and guttural. Was this Mrs. Fischer? I rose in the elevator to the tenth floor, found myself outside a door with an elaborate knocker in the shape of a mermaid.

The door was answered when I knocked by the owner of the voice, a tall, white-haired woman in a black dress and a maid's starched white cap and apron. She indicated in her rather limited English that I should wait in the living-room, and I sat down gingerly on the edge of a brocaded sofa. My wait was not long—after all I should have been there fifteen minutes earlier. The maid returned, and led me into an inner office where Eva Fischer faced me across her desk. A woman no longer young, though I could not place what her age might be. Somewhere in her fifties, perhaps? Her hair was still dark, and she had kept her figure; but the lines on her forehead and around her mouth must have been cut by age or grief, or perhaps by both. Her cheekbones were high and prominent, and had been somewhat accentuated by rouge. She had also taken some care with the eyebrows which curved over what were still fine lustrous dark eyes. A woman who had been pretty in her day, and was still not without her attractions.

"Thank you, Else, you may go," she said to the maid, who withdrew discreetly, closing the door softly behind her.

Mrs. Fischer indicated a chair opposite her, and I sat down. "You are late, Miss Summers," she said to me rather formally and with a touch of severity.

I explained that I had lost my way. Her look expressed disbelief, although it was less severe. I found myself disliking her. I was not sure what I had expected, but I had not expected this middle-aged Teutonic woman who doubted my word and who was critical of me for being late when I knew I was always early.

However, now that she had shown her disapproval of lateness, her manner became more kindly and she set out to put me at my ease by asking those routine questions one expects in doctors' offices. Eventually she asked a question which was, for me, less routine, though I suppose it was routine enough for her. "Have you ever had help of this kind before?" she asked.

I hesitated. Did I like her well enough to tell her the truth? It wasn't a question of liking. I had to trust her, because I did not know if I could find anyone else. "Only once," I told her hesitantly, "from a psychiatrist in a hospital just after I had tried to kill myself."

To my relief, she did not look upset or even much interested. "And why did you do that, Kate? I may call you Kate?"

"Because I was fond of someone who married someone else," I said, telling one part of the truth.

To my surprise, she laughed. She had a pleasant, musical infectious laugh, and I almost, in my astonishment, laughed with her.

"You must excuse me," she said. "Believe me, I know it is serious. But it is your English understatement that is funny. You are fond—only a little fond—of someone, and you try to kill yourself when he marries someone else? You must see that it is funny."

Perhaps I might like her, just a little, after all.

The interview did not last long. "You must understand," she said, "that if you come late you will have a shorter session. I have another patient coming. Next time, you come on Saturday morning, at ten AM. On time."

I had not been altogether certain that I would come for another interview, but decided after all I might as well.

Within two weeks I was writing in my diary that I felt much better, that my headaches were going away, that perhaps I might complete the treatment within a few months. I had almost forgotten my initial dislike of Mrs. Fischer. I had never known anyone who was such a good listener, who was so ready to accept all those details of childhood guilt and misery. After the first few sessions, the chair I had sat in disappeared, and I lay on the analyst's couch of all those cartoons, staring at a painting (I seem to remember a beach scene with blue water and white sand, but I am not sure) and talking to Mrs. Fischer as she sat beside me. Sometimes I was disconcerted when I looked up by chance and found her either too interested or not interested enough; usually her eyes were half-closed, and she wore what I thought of as her hooded look.

What I told her then no longer matters. It is Eva Fischer

I am trying to understand, not myself. I suppose those accounts of childhood troubles must have been fairly routine for her; she must have been bored at times. No doubt she was well enough aware fairly soon in the process that the analysis would take longer than the three or four months I had so optimistically predicted. No doubt she knew I would be worse before I was better. She was not, I suppose, surprised by my dependency, the period when I was clinging to her and found it hard to live between sessions. She tried to explain to me the nature of transfer, that I felt for her as a child feels when it is separated from its mother, or a woman when she is separated from her lover.

All children feel curious at some time about their parents. If I told her everything, I also wanted to know some things about her. Who was this Mrs. Fischer, the Mrs. F. of my diary? Where did she come from? What had her life been before she came to Canada.

I put together, piece by piece, information, as one puts together the pieces of a jigsaw puzzle. She was the widow, I learned, of a writer, an Austrian Jewish novelist whom I had never heard of, but who Mrs. F. told me had been well known in his time and place. She herself had been the daughter of a wealthy Viennese family, not Jewish. She and her husband had taken refuge from Hitler in Switzerland, and after her husband's death she had come out to Canada with her daughter, who was now grown-up and living in New York. Yes, she had been psychoanalyzed by the great Jung himself during her life in Switzerland.

I couldn't think why she would have been psychoanalyzed, except out of curiosity. Aside from that flight from Hitler, I thought her life sounded happy enough, in the small glimpses she gave me to illustrate some point she was making about my own life. There was an idyllic childhood in Vienna, with her adored parents—especially her adored father—and her older brother, the brother who had later become an actor in America. She had been a lively and talented girl, had acquired some reputation as an artist. Some of the paintings on the walls were her own, although she no longer painted. Her marriage, although to a man much older than herself, sounded happy. She had obviously adored Josef Fischer, considered him one of the great talents of the age, and clearly supposed (though she did not say so in so many words) that my reason for not knowing his work was the backwardness, the rusticity of a little city like Ottawa.

My curiosity about the Fischers could not have been as great as it later became, for I did not immediately try to hunt up Josef Fischer's books. Perhaps Mrs. Fischer discouraged me. Did she say that they were for the most part badly translated? Or was it just that I lacked the energy, in the early days of the analysis, to find my way to a library that might have translations of his work? I was wrapped up in my own concerns, of course, and was chiefly interested in Mrs. Fischer's marriage as a model for some hypothetical marriage I might make myself. Might I possibly, like Eva Fischer, marry a famous author older than myself? Was marriage especially difficult for a woman with talents? I thought of myself as a writer although at present I could not seem to write. Mrs. Fischer had been a painter, was obviously a woman of intelligence. Yet she seemed to have been rather domestic, to have enjoyed looking after husband and child. I was delighted by the model of married harmony that she provided for me. Might I also manage to have the best of all worlds—be a writer myself, sympathize with the career of a brilliant and charming husband, and at the same time cook nourishing meals for my lively children? Before this time, I had been rather contemptuous of women who were interested in their houses or in their own appearance.

Yet it was clear that Mrs. Fischer thought these matters were not unworthy of attention. Not to care about appearances, she seemed to suggest, might mean that one didn't respect the selfhood behind the appearance. "How can a young woman who thinks she wants to marry not bother powdering her nose?" she inquired of me one day, rather acidly. Ah, Mrs. F., Mrs. F.! I suppose she was old-fashioned. Or was she?

It was autumn when I first started going to see Mrs. F. I dreaded Christmas, when she went away to New York for a couple of weeks. She seemed to realize my almost childish dread of her absence, and, instead of our usual session of analysis, invited me into her living-room for cake and wine. She had put up a little Christmas tree with wax candles, and gave me a present, a Mexican pendant with blue stones. I still have it, at the back of a drawer somewhere, although something has happened to the chain.

When she came back she talked of the relatives she had visited, her brother, about whom she worried because he had a heart condition, and her daughter. I was surprised that she mentioned disagreeing with her daughter at times. Her family life was not quite perfect, then? I was also, as my dreams at the time showed, pleased that she did not always agree with the daughter. "Family jealousy, Katie," she said to me teasingly. "You want to be my favourite child."

I found a novel of Josef Fischer's in the nearest branch of the Public Library and read it but did not like it. I tried to explain to Mrs. Fischer why I did not like it. "It was too romantic," I said, "too Gothic. I like solid, sensible novels with real details in them."

"Your tastes are incorrigibly English," she said. "Or is it that you are jealous of Josef too as well as of my daughter?"

Perhaps she was right. I began to be afraid, to be panicky

about the kind of relationship that was developing.

"Don't worry, Kate," she said soothingly. "They all feel like that, all the patients. It's not really me you're attached to. Tell me who else you've been jealous of."

The winter passed. As spring gradually and grudgingly approached, I sometimes walked to Mrs. Fischer's instead of taking the streetcar. Some days come back to me: a cold, windy March day, for instance, when there has been snow and rain. A wind blows through the trees, which are full of little particles of ice that make a strange noise, as though pellets of glass were being rubbed against one another. There is a glare of ice underfoot, grey and glossy. While I am at Mrs. Fischer's a storm of thick, soft, wet snow comes up. I walk home through it, unable to see my way across the street. The ground becomes mushy rather than icy. There is a sense of release about that soft, blinding snow, connected with the ease of tension at the back of my neck just after I have talked to Mrs. Fischer. I come home weary, ready to curl up on top of my bed and fall asleep.

Or it is early summer. An Ottawa heat wave. Mrs. F. is planning to visit Vienna, for the first time in many years, and is trying to prepare me for her absence. I sense that she is already partly absent. What are those memories, of Vienna, of Zurich, that she returns to?

I myself go off for a solitary holiday in a small Laurentian resort. I walk daily to the village, where I sit in the small toy-like church with its clutter of candles and statuary. I stare at the crucifix, half praying, half letting my mind drift around past and future. Then I walk back to the Lodge, sit on the sundeck in a bathing suit and sunglasses, reading another book by Josef Fischer. I like this better than the one I read before, but am disappointed that I cannot see anyone in the book who resembles Eva Fischer.

When we had both returned to Ottawa again, the analysis seemed stuck in a sort of doldrums area. We circled around and around the same events in the past, the same problems. I seemed even to have the same dreams. I had a feeling of not having reached deep enough into my private world; at the same time I felt that Mrs. F. (or was it myself?) was directing me outward, to external practical problems. Should I get an apartment away from my parents so as to ease the strain at home? Should I attempt to find a job that would interest me more than the one I had?

One session, when we had seemed to be making more progress than we had for a time, we were interrupted by the paper boy wanting money. To my surprise, Mrs. Fischer scolded him very vigorously. He had been told not to interrupt her at this hour. He was a stupid young oaf. I felt that she was making too much fuss, and a critical expression must have shown on my face. "As usual, Katie," she said angrily to me, "you expect perfection. It would do you good if you lost your temper now and then at your parents or your detestable boss. I at least am not to be fitted into that kind of mould. He was not to come on a day when Else isn't here to answer him. I cannot have my work interrupted."

I agreed that I was too anxious for perfection, that I had, as Mrs. Fischer would have sometimes said, an overdeveloped superego, or, as a priest might have said, an excess of scruples. I did seem to demand of myself that I should always be sweet, gentle, and compliant, as well as very competent; that I should keep all the commandments, even the minor ones. (Mrs. F. said that I was a Baptist Catholic.) I knew that such a demand for self-perfection could prevent me from doing anything or gaining anything. I hesitated to write a poem for fear it might be flawed or to make a friendship for fear it might be a failure. Was I applying the same sort of standard to Mrs. Fischer? Surely she had the right to lose her temper at the paper boy? Yes, but not to shout at him, I thought.

Time passed, another autumn, another winter. I moved away from my parents into a bachelor apartment with a couch, a lamp, and a card table. I made a few friends. I played at cooking and keeping house. I did a little writing. I had a new job at the Public Library.

It was there, in flipping through a reference book on twentieth-century authors, that I found an entry on Josef Fischer. Why had I not looked it up before? Had I been incurious, or had I felt that I ought not to trespass on Eva's earlier life? (By this time I called her Eva, in my mind at least. She was still Mrs. Fischer when I talked to her.) Josef Fischer was, as Mrs. Fischer had said, an author of considerable reputation with a long list of novels and biographies to his credit. What about his personal life? A few years after the first Great War, the notice said, he had been separated from his wife Selma, by whom he had had several children. After his tragic separation from her (why was it tragic?) his companion had been the painter and illustrator Eva Wiebe, by whom he had also had a daughter. They had lived in Switzerland, where he had died in 1940.

I was startled by this information. Had Eva not, after all, been married to Josef Fischer? What did that word "companion" mean? If she had been married to Josef Fischer, how could she, as a Catholic, marry a divorced man? What were these implications of "tragic" circumstances? In her picture of a happy marriage (which I felt was intended as a model for a possible life of my own) there had not seemed to be room in the background for another wife and children, perhaps deserted on Eva's account. I felt that my image of Eva had been shattered, and along with it my view of the kind of person I ought to become and the kind of life I ought to lead.

What seemed especially upsetting, when I thought of it, was that Eva had not told me the truth. I had told her everything about myself; and although I had not expected her to tell me everything in return, I had not expected her to tell me lies. Surely, though, "lies" was too strong a word? Even though she might not have been legally married to Josef Fischer, she had lived with him for many years and had borne him a daughter. Baptist Catholic though she might call me, I was not so conventional as to suppose all marriages were made in church before priests.

I was not due to see her for several days. However, after spending a disturbed night, I telephoned her, as I had rarely done. What in the world had I been reading, she asked? Yes, Josef had had an earlier, unhappy marriage, made when he was only twenty-two. Frau Selma Fischer had been a difficult, indeed an abnormal person, and the marriage had not worked. There had been problems with her and with the children, though Eva had looked after the youngest child herself. It had been a difficult life in many ways, but certainly not one to be ashamed of. She would tell me more when I came in for the next interview.

When I arrived after work on Monday for my interview, I found her looking tired and worn. She had put on a black dress and had omitted her usual make-up. She was alone; it was one of Else's days off. She arose to greet me, as she did not usually do, and took my hand in both of hers. Looking earnestly into my eyes, she said, "I wish I could know what goes on in that funny little head of yours, Kate. Why are you so upset by all this? It's my tragedy, not yours. Why do you think I should have worried you with it? Am I not entitled to a life of my own, to my own past?"

"Yes—yes, of course you are. But still it is partly my business. If I went to a surgeon to have my appendix out, his character wouldn't matter, only his hands and his skill. But you aren't just operating on my appendix. It's my mind, my soul even. I have to trust you, you see."

"Can't you still trust me? I haven't lied to you; I've just omitted to tell you some truths which I didn't think concerned you. Do you think I am an evil woman? I am only an unlucky one."

"Of course I don't think you are evil. But I thought of you as my model for a happy life. I wanted to be like you. Now I'm not sure."

"I see what you mean. People imitate their parents' marriage, and I have become a second mother to you. It was a good marriage; it had its trials, but it was a true friendship to the end, and it was not at anyone's expense, whatever Selma Fischer said. I did not ruin her marriage. She ruined it herself, before I ever met Josef."

She told me the story of herself and Selma and Josef, of Selma's half-insane jealousy both before and after the divorce, of the perpetual lawsuits with which she pestered her ex-husband. The figure of Selma which she presented seemed bizarre, extravagant. Could I believe her? Was Selma unbalanced to the point of evil, or was she only pathetic and neurotic? Eva must be telling the truth; the conviction of sincerity was in every word she said. And yet Eva's truth and Selma's truth were probably different.

Did she not have some pity for Selma, this half-crazy suicidal woman?

Of course she pitied her, she tried to understand her. But it was not just a mild neurosis, I must understand. "You are seeing her as like yourself," she said, glancing at me shrewdly. "You are wrong, of course. You are sane and reasonable—maybe too sane and reasonable. You are neurotic, you have your problems, you get depressed or maybe tense; but there is nothing wrong with your reason, your power of understanding. Believe me, you are not at all like Selma. You would not, if your lover or husband left you, come half-clad howling at his door like some kind of wild animal."

I laughed. "Of course you laugh at the idea," she said. "So would I. You are more like me than like her, after all. You must not go over to her side, Kate. She turned enough people against me there in Europe. Why should she turn you against me now because you have read a silly paragraph in a book?"

She was right, of course. I was not turned against her. But I could no longer see her as someone infinitely strong, wise, and joyous, placed above the storm of circumstance. She too had been unsure of herself. She too had suffered scruples of conscience. She too had lain awake all night worrying. She too was sometimes ungenerous. She too told half-truths. She too, in short, was imperfect.

That was, I suppose, a turning-point in the analysis. I never depended on Eva to quite the same extent again, and yet at times I felt closer to her than I had before. After all, I now knew something about her. Not long after that, her brother in New York died of a sudden heart attack, and once more I saw her stricken. Which of us was helping the other, I wondered, when I saw her visibly grieving? My own troubles seemed somehow smaller than hers.

I continued seeing her for my remaining six months in Ottawa, although less frequently in the later months. Then I moved to Toronto to work. I went to see her before leaving town, a mute, embarrassed farewell session, like the farewells in railway stations. For a time in Toronto I had periods when I missed her greatly. Once or twice I came to Ottawa for a weekend and had lunch or tea with her. These occasions were pleasant; we talked to each other politely about movies or books or art exhibitions. But across a table in a restaurant we no longer seemed to be quite the same people.

Then I had a period when things went wrong for me again, and I found myself blaming Eva. Had I somehow been shortchanged in my analysis so that I was not able to cope with an emergency? On one visit to Ottawa I met her on the street but failed to recognize her until she was past and did not speak to her. (How could I fail to recognize her?) She did not see me, or did not appear to see me. Yet I still remember her face as I glimpsed it then, half smiling.

Ten years after the analysis was over I heard she was dead, had died suddenly of a heart attack on a visit to Vienna. So her widowhood was over. My own parents were dead; I was no longer a Catholic; I had never made that ideal marriage I had imagined for myself. But I still sometimes heard Eva's voice in my ear, though I did not always agree with what it said. I no longer thought her a bad analyst because my life had not been ideally happy. Why should it be? I had gone on living. I had even gone on writing. She would have been satisfied, I thought.

Lately, after all these years, I have been looking again at Josef Fischer's novels, especially that last novel he wrote, the autobiographical one. I don't remember reading it before. Was it not in the Ottawa Public Library? Was it one of the novels that Eva told me was badly translated? It is really, I discover, quite a powerful novel, though an uneven one. It tells the story of the unhappy marriage of a famous German novelist. Bertha, the novelist's first wife, is rather like Selma as Eva had portrayed her to me. And yet she has in her youth an odd charm, an absurdity that is almost lovable until she turns into a witch and ogress. She is the character who makes the book live. And then there is Johanna, the young woman who is first the hero's mistress (does

Fischer use that word, or is it Bertha's?) and then his second wife. Johanna is affectionate, gentle, courageous, loyal. She is a talented musician. I recognize her high cheekbones, her dark liquid eyes, her laugh. But can Johanna be Eva? She has no temper. She is all sweetness. She is too perfect. Did Josef Fischer not understand Eva? Did I understand Eva? Did she understand herself?

And what about Kate Summers? If I have never understood Eva, do I understand Kate?